12, 27, 44, 59, 64,
98, 129

Finding the Way
in AD 100

Finding the Way in AD 100

A story from the early days of Christianity

by
Roger Kirby

Books written simply & clearly to help you think, learn and grow!

pulp theology .co.uk

www.pulptheology.co.uk

Acknowledgements

With grateful thanks to my computer guru, mentor and editor: Dave Roberts

Finding the Way in AD 100 – version 1.1

Text Copyright © 2015 Roger Kirby

ISBN-13: 978-1519433466
ISBN-10: 1519433468

Cover photo is of the Hierapolis - Ephesus Way built by the ancient Romans.

Dedication

To my beloved wife Margaret

1

It was two years since Trajan became the Roman Caesar, thirty years since the total destruction of Jerusalem by Titus, and sixty-seven years since the death and resurrection of Jesus of Nazareth[1] (we would call it AD 100). None of these three major events had been of any significance to the young man slowly trudging up the track to the top of the pass, though one of them soon would be.

He realized he was there at last. There was no higher ground in front of him, so it must be the top of the pass, and he could look forward to some downhill walking to the village he was going to. He was not used to walking so far in one day for he was a city boy and he was seldom so far from his home in Sidon. His muscles were tired and sore. His feet had taken a battering on the rough ground for all the high quality of the Roman road surfaces. His sandals were stout enough but small stones had crept under his feet and caused bruises, blisters and cuts.

He had walked with a caravan of camels along the main highway to the foot of the pass. It was better to be in company for there were plenty of bandits around in spite of the presence of many Roman soldiers in the country. The leader of the caravan had assured him that he would see the village that was his destination from the top of this ridge but there was no sign of it as yet. He walked on across the nearly level ground of the broad summit between the boulders and over the dry parched ground longing for a sight of greenery and houses signalling the end of his journey.

ˌAt last he came to the point where the path left the level area and started to go down zigzagging backwards and forwards to ease the way. The descent was quite steep and, as he looked down, he could see trees, fields and some houses that were clearly part of a village most of which was still hidden from sight under the hill. That must be his destination.

There were, as usual, steep short cuts across each bend of the winding track and he was still young enough not to refuse the challenge of these paths. He was down three of them, his knees aching, and wondering whether he should take it more gently when his eye caught movement below him. He stopped to see more clearly what it was. Nearly a full kilometre below him he could see someone running fast towards the track he was on. Then he realised there were two other figures some distance behind but obviously pursuing the first figure. He watched, intrigued. He sat down, enjoying the excuse for a rest.

A moment later he jumped up. The first figure was a woman or a girl? He could not see the others clearly at first as they were behind a group of small trees, but then as they came out into the open he realized they were two men and by the size and bulk of them not young either. He hesitated. If this were an innocent chase he would look a fool if he did anything. If it wasn't it was never wise to interfere in other people's quarrels. The men might be armed with knives or swords and he had neither, only a stout staff. What should he do?

Then he thought he heard a cry, a shout of distress. He decided the least he could do was get closer to where they were so that anything that was going to happen had to happen in front of a stranger – himself. He could at least be a witness if there was any malicious intent on the part of the men. Tiredness and aching knees forgotten he set off at top speed down the hill. He went fast down the short cuts, leaping, jumping and sliding, keeping his balance only with great difficulty.

At first there was no reaction from those below him. The

girl continued running fast along the banks between the small terraced fields where the hill was less steep, the men following and gaining rapidly on her. But then he stumbled and sent several large stones crashing down the hill in front of him. The girl heard and looked up, saw him, hesitated for a moment, and then changed her direction heading up hill towards him. That saved her. He could now see that she was much younger than the men and that she was at least as fast as them uphill.

The men looked up and, seeing him, hesitated in their running. His knees and muscles were burning so he had to slow down himself. At an impulse he put his staff, which was fairly heavy, across his shoulders and rested his arms on it so that it was clearly visible. That did it. The two men stopped and started to walk away in the opposite direction. The girl stopped running but continued walking fast towards the track until she was close enough to see him clearly. Then she too stopped. She was clearly trying to work out who he was and how friendly he was.

Whatever it was she saw in him she decided it was safe to continue and recommenced walking towards the track and him. He hailed her. She nodded her head and came on. He could see she was red in the face, gasping for breath and finding it hard to even walk as the tension and the adrenalin drained out of her.

She reached the track and sat down on a boulder beside it, huddled over trying to get her breath and her composure back, waiting for him to come down to her.

"Who are you?" was the first thing she said, between the gasps for breath, with challenge and emphasis in her voice.

"Gaius Severus."

"Where are you from? I haven't seen you before, have I? What are you doing here?"

He couldn't help smiling at her and all her questions.

"I'm from Sidon. You haven't seen me before. I have

come to see someone in the village. Any more questions?"

His good humour and ready smile helped her to begin to relax.

"I'm sorry. I have to thank you very much for coming down the hill like that. I don't know what would have happened if they had caught me."

"You mean you didn't know them at all? Who they were or where they came from?"

"No. They are not from anywhere around here. They may have been slavers or something. I hate to think what might have happened had you not been around."

Gaius had been busy trying to assess the girl. She looked highly competent, strong, good looking and older than he had at first thought, probably about his age. Good girls did not talk to strange men like this but he reckoned that the circumstances were sufficiently exceptional to be a good excuse. She noticed his gaze, flushed, and tried to straighten out her dishevelled clothing and her head covering which had slipped down onto her shoulders.

Gaius wondered whether he should breach normal good manners and ask her name.

Before he could do so she volunteered it "I am Anna. I cannot thank you enough for what you did. You said you were coming to our village. Who were you coming to see?"

"A man called Jacob Ben Joseph," he replied, and then, watching closely to see what her reaction would be, "the Christian, the follower of Jesus of Nazareth."

He was rewarded with the broadest of broad smiles and the simple statement, "he is my grandfather. Our house is in the village. Let's walk down to it and I will introduce you to him. He is a wonderful man."

They started off down the track. Gaius was puzzled about what had happened. "Surely you weren't out in the country all by yourself?" he asked, "I wouldn't have thought that was safe even in an area like this."

"No, of course not. I was with a friend and her two boys. We were gathering wild pomegranates. I must have wandered away from the others and got out of sight of them, when those two awful men came up to me. Fortunately I could run faster than they could, at least for a while."

She stopped suddenly with a cry of dismay. "Oh! I must go and tell my friends I am all right and find my basket again. I had quite forgotten." And then, after a pause, "Please, will you come with me?"

He grinned at her. "Of course. I don't really think I should let you go wandering off by yourself!"

She couldn't help smiling back. "Don't be horrid." And before he could reply went off to the side along a faint track between two fields. He followed her as she went swiftly along first one track then another, jumping the irrigation channels in between. She followed an erratic course for some time but keeping the same direction, reversing the way he had seen her running in the first place. She stopped, called out, and listened for a reply, which came faintly from behind a small group of trees. She went that way and in a moment they came within sight of an older woman and two fairly large boys.

The presence of Gaius behind her caused obvious surprise and required considerable explanation, as did the events that had occurred out of sight of this group. There were many expressions of horror at what had happened and explanations to Gaius that this sort of thing had not previously happened in this area. It was enough to bring the fruit gathering expedition to an end. Anna retrieved her basket from where she had dropped it and most of the fruit that had fallen out of it. The five of them set off towards the village.

Before long the family group branched off to one side leaving Anna and Gaius on a more direct route towards the village.

They continued down towards the village, not quite knowing what to say to each other. It was not at all usual for a fellow and a girl who did not know each other to be walking together. As they approached the village Gaius broke the silence, "Hadn't you better put your head covering up now we are getting near the houses, or people will wonder whatever you are doing?"

Anna was clearly quite confused and distraught by all that had happened by now, but she welcomed his concern and tidied herself up as much as possible. She led the way swiftly up to the first row of houses, round a corner and in at an open gateway. Gaius saw that it was a bigger house than many of those nearby. The gateway opened into a courtyard with rooms round three sides and a way through to back premises. He noticed that there were signs that many horses or mules had passed through the courtyard to that area so it was obviously a working house.

Anna led him across the courtyard to the far end where there was movement under a large walnut tree. As Gaius got closer he could see that there was an old man sitting in the deep shade. He was old, very old. His face was all lined and wrinkled but his eyes were bright and twinkling, suggesting an active and lively mind. He naturally looked very surprised to see his granddaughter coming into the house with a completely strange man and raised his eyebrows waiting for an explanation. Anna scarcely knew where to begin.

"Grandpa," she burst out, "this is Gaius, from Sidon. He saved me from two men who were trying to catch me. He has been so, so, kind to me."

The release of tension proved too much for her and she burst into tears, much to the surprise of both Gaius and Grandfather Jacob. Gaius felt very uncomfortable. Jacob examined them both very closely.

"Come, my dear," he said to Anna, "I can see that something very distressing has happened and this young man had something to do with it. Sit down, and tell me all about it."

Anna stifled her sobs and quickly regained her usual composure. The whole story came pouring out. Gaius had to explain where he came from and how he fitted into the story. Jacob was very shocked by what he heard and confirmed what the others had said about nothing like this having happened in the area before.

He pointed out that they would need to warn the rest of the villagers about what had happened and that none of the women and girls should go out unaccompanied for at least some time to come. Gaius could see that although he was old he was very assured in his reactions and decisions. He thanked Gaius profusely for what he had done. He asked Anna to bring drink and food out for them all to eat. As they ate and chatted together something more like normality returned. Anna explained that Gaius had come to see him. So he turned to Gaius and said "now, young man, what can I do for you? Tell me about yourself."

"I am Gaius Severus from the city of Sidon, in Phoenicia."

The old man raised his eyebrows. "You have a Greek name, but you speak Aramaic, as we do, though with an accent that suggests it is not your mother tongue. How does that come about?"

"My father is Greek, but my mother came from Judaea. They have lived and worked in all sorts of places as they traded round the Great Sea. I was given a Greek name, learned good Greek in the city and some Aramaic at home from my mother. But I have not used it much recently so my Aramaic is not all that good – as you will have noticed. Do you speak Greek?"

Jacob immediately switched from the Aramaic they had

been speaking and answered, "Yes" in Greek. "I am happy to speak in Greek, but I am not sure my Greek is any better than your Aramaic. We shall probably be able to understand each other very well if we speak the language we are most comfortable with or even mix them up as we go along. Why are you here and what can I do for you?"

"Well, sir, thank you very much. It is a very long story. "

"Not to worry. I can afford to sit and listen as long as you like. I am old now and my family looks after me exceedingly well. Tell me your story."

Gaius hesitated, trying to get his thoughts in order before he spoke. "I suppose it all started as I finished my studies at the schools of philosophy and rhetoric. I was supposed to go on to be a Rabbi[2] but for some reason, I don't really know why, my parents sent me to the Greek schools first. There they filled my head with so many complicated arguments that I began to question the faith that my mother had taught me. I soon gave up studying the Torah because I was becoming less and less convinced it was the right way to live my life.

Then I started to meet some people who called themselves - or rather other people called them - Christians. They told some astonishing stories about a man called Jesus. They claimed he was the Chosen One of God, the Messiah, or Christ as we say in Greek. They had many stories about him that seemed to me quite incredible. They claimed he healed people, he made blind people see, and he even brought some dead people back to life. They said he was executed by crucifixion by the Romans but that should surely have meant that he was just another one of the many men who have claimed to be the Messiah in the last few years but have been shown to have failed in their claims. They then made the monstrous claim that he came back to life again and was seen by many people. I find that very hard to believe."

"Let me interrupt for a moment," said Jacob. "It is easy to guess that you have come all this way because I am known to be a Christian. Why have you gone to all this trouble if you think the stories those people told are so ridiculous?"

"Well," said Gaius, his brow knitted in a troubled frown, "partly, I suppose, it is sheer curiosity, but more than that I think it is because although the stories these Christians told seemed so strange and unbelievable they, themselves, are the very opposite of ridiculous. They are living good lives. They are happier that most other people in Sidon. They are patient, they are kind; they are contented with life even when they have very little to be contented with. The rich people among them are treating poor people well, talking to them, helping them, being friendly with them in a very unusual way. Husbands and wives are getting on well together with the men treating the women in a kind and good way. They all seem to be just plain good. And that in spite of the fact that some of them were quite notorious characters in the town before they became Christians."

Jacob smiled. "That is good to hear," he said. "What can I do to help, then?"

"I am full of questions! Some of them, I think, very hard questions. The Christians in Sidon struggled to answer them in a way that I found satisfactory. That was probably because they could only tell me what they had heard themselves. But I want answers. And I am sure the very best answers will come from someone who was actually an eyewitness of the events that involved this man, Jesus. When I asked around where I might get answers, and where I could get answers from an eyewitness, it is your name that I kept on getting. So when my father wanted me to go to Caesarea[3] and I realized this village is not far off the main road to there I asked him if I might stop here to see you. He said 'yes' so here I am. Full of questions."

Chapter 1

"What did you hear about me?" asked Jacob, trying not to look too pleased with this description of himself.

"I heard that you knew Jesus when he was alive, that you are one of the few people still living who claim to have seen Jesus alive after he was executed, that, although you are a village man, you are very good at giving sensible and honest answers to awkward questions, and saying you don't know when you don't know!"

"Well, I don't know about the sensible answers – you must judge that. As for saying I don't know when I don't know I will certainly do that. Jesus said we must always tell the truth. We are not even to confirm what we say by an oath. Even more important he said he was 'the Way, and the Truth and the Life'.[4] I know some people think it is more important to keep people happy by telling them what they want to hear but Jesus clearly set his face against doing that. To him truth was more important than anybody's feelings or desires. Truth is hugely important.

As for the other thing you said: I certainly did see Jesus after he died and indeed he was not dead but alive and well! I didn't really know Jesus before his crucifixion, though I had seen him. I was only a boy on a day I have never forgotten when Jesus took the lunch my mother had given me and fed a great crowd of people with it[5]. I did get to know Philip and Andrew, two of his closest disciples, as a result of that day and later on they told me a lot more about Jesus than I had been able to see or hear for myself.

You must stay with us until we have finished with all your questions. If you are not too tired with your journey we can start right now. There is still some time before supper."

"Thank you very much, sir. I will be delighted to stay with you. I am tired but I am also very excited to be here, and keen to start talking about all the things that puzzle me. I cannot stay for long though, perhaps two nights at the most. I have business in Caesarea."

"That is settled then," said Jacob. He turned and called over his shoulder towards the house, "Anna."

"Yes, granddad. What is it?" she said as she came into view in the doorway of one of the rooms.

"This young man is staying with us, for two nights. Tell your mother, please, and ask her to get the spare room ready. Oh, and make sure she has enough for a guest tonight when we sit down to eat."

"Right, granddad, but mother is not here. Have you forgotten? She has gone to Aunt Joanna's for most of the week. I will be happy to do everything myself" she said with a smile and a dimple, that Gaius thought most attractive, as she went back into the house.

"Oh! Yes," said Jacob, looking annoyed with himself, "I had forgotten." Then to Gaius, "Come, the air is getting quite chilly. Let's move to those seats over there where we can catch the last of the sun and start." He struggled to get to his feet, and after a moment's hesitation Gaius jumped across to help him up. Jacob smiled his thanks and moved slowly across the courtyard to where there was a couch with cushions. He carefully lowered himself into place and beckoned to Gaius to sit beside him. "Now, young man, where shall we start?"

2

Gaius thought hard, his forehead creasing into a frown. "Well, sir. I think I would like to leave you to choose where we start. What do you think is the most important single thing about Jesus?"

Jacob smiled. "That is an easy question to answer. It is the fact that Jesus rose again from the dead. He was resurrected."

"What does that mean, resurrection?"

"It means that somebody comes back to life again after they have died, to live for ever. The prophet Ezekiel spoke about it a long time ago when he had a vision of the dead people of Israel coming back to life again in the valley of the dry bones. Ever since then we have had the hope that this will happen. What we expected to happen was that all the dead people would rise again at the same time, not that one person would rise ahead of all the rest. That is what happened to Jesus. He was dead and put in a tomb. Then he came back to life."

Gaius's frown deepened. "But that is the most impossible thing of all that is said about him. Dead men do not rise and live again. They stay dead. Everyone knows that. Whatever happened Jesus cannot have risen from the dead. Such things simply do not happen."

"I quite agree. Dead men do not rise to resurrection life. I know. We know. It does not happen. It cannot happen. It will not happen. But it did happen. Once!"

"But how can you say that. The totally impossible does not happen. What makes you want to say that it did happen?"

Jacob drew a deep breath. "Let me tell you what happened the day Jesus died and two days later, as I know it.

Jesus died on a Friday afternoon.[6] Two men, who were rich, had influence and had been following Jesus, asked the authorities for his body. They were given it, and put it in a tomb, which belonged to one of them.[7] There was nothing very special about the tomb. It happened to be new and conveniently close to where Jesus was executed. The following day was the Saturday Sabbath so, of course, nothing was done then.

Early the next day a group of women went to the tomb because they wanted to clean and tidy up his body, embalm it and do all the things that should have been done to his brutally mangled body but were not because of the hurry to get him buried.[8] They knew an armed guard had been set on the tomb by the authorities to make sure nobody stole the body but they thought that they ought to be able to get permission to go in since they were women. When they got there the guard was nowhere to be seen and the tomb was open, the stone at the entrance having been rolled away. They went in and were surprised to find his body was not there. Then one of them met a man in the garden where the tomb was and to her initial disbelief and total amazement recognised him as Jesus.[9] The women all hurried back to where the rest of the disciples of Jesus had gathered together and told them what had happened.[10]

When Jacob stopped speaking for a moment Gaius broke into his story. "But that is already a rather impossible story to believe. The witnesses to the empty tomb and to Jesus being around were women! Surely you do not believe them? We Greeks might think they were telling the truth but you country folk would never accept the testimony of women!"

Jacob replied, "Hold on a minute. I am going on to tell you how men immediately went to check the truth of what they were saying, and found it all to be as they said.

But let me point out that what happened was completely in line with the way Jesus treated women. He would have accepted their testimony as he would have accepted a man's. It was women that were involved first according to all the accounts of what happened. As soon as they brought the news of the empty tomb the two leaders of his disciples ran out to the tomb to see what had happened.[11]

They were as surprised and as disbelieving as the women were – and as you are – for exactly the same reason. Such things do not happen. But they did. All the disciples saw Jesus at least once each after that. Peter, the leading disciple, had several conversations with him. James, a member of Jesus' family, saw him too although he had not been a very close follower of Jesus up to that point.

A few days later a meeting of people who had been following Jesus during his ministry was called in Galilee to discuss what was happening, and try to work out what it all meant and, to everyone's utter astonishment, Jesus appeared in the middle of the meeting and spoke to it himself. There were more than 500 people there, watching and listening to him[12]."

Jacob paused, and a strange look came over his face. He said very quietly so that Gaius had to strain to hear him, "I saw Jesus. I was there myself. I saw Jesus alive. I saw the resurrected Jesus. I saw the first and only man to conquer death. I know, because I saw him!"

Jacob was obviously so overcome by his memory that Gaius did not know what to say next. After a pause he said, very hesitantly, "I understand something of what that must mean to you, sir. But I want to know for myself. Do you mind if I cross-examine you about this? It is an extraordinary story and not easily believed. I do not want to say that you are wrong but I cannot accept what you say without question. If this is true it changes a lot of things."

Jacob's face and manner returned to normal. "I know. I

understand," he said, "Jesus himself said there would be a special blessing in heaven for those who have not seen him but yet have believed.[13] So you can get a bigger blessing than I ever got – though I am quite happy with mine! Go on with your questions and I will answer them as best I can."

Gaius paused and thought for a long time before saying anything. Jacob waited patiently.

"Perhaps Jesus did not really die, but people thought he had? He was taken down from the cross in a state of shock and unconsciousness. Then he revived after he had been put in the tomb and walked out to go and stay somewhere else in Jerusalem, only appearing to the disciples on specially chosen occasions. That could easily have happened. There is no need to talk about returning from the dead and resurrection at all."

He made this last statement with an air of triumph, clearly thinking that he had solved the problem.

Jacob frowned, "Have you ever seen a Roman crucifixion close to?" he asked.

Gaius shook his head. "No. Of course not. They are not the sort of thing that one goes looking out for. I always hurry past anywhere there has been a crucifixion. They are not at all pleasant."

"Yes, that is what I expected you to answer. If you had seen one close up you would know that what you suggest could not possibly have happened. I have seen one close up. I made myself do so simply to convince myself that what you suggest is impossible. Think about it for a moment. Jesus was more than half dead before he even got to the place of crucifixion. He had been beaten with what the Romans called the 'verberatio', the most terrible form of scourging, with the whips having pieces of bone and metal in the thongs. His whole back will have been a mess of blood and torn flesh by the time they finished. You would have been able to see some of the bones of his back where all the flesh had been ripped off.

Men often die under that sort of scourging before they can be taken to be crucified. Then he was nailed to the cross through his hands or wrists and the bones of his feet. If he had been found to be alive after he was taken down from the cross the soldiers responsible for the execution would have been executed themselves – the same way. You can be quite sure they would be very careful not to make any mistakes. Indeed we know that Jesus had his side torn open by one of the soldiers with his spear just to make sure that he was thoroughly and completely dead.[14] It is totally impossible to think that he could have survived.

There are two other things to consider. First, he could not naturally have reappeared only two days after the crucifixion. It would have taken any man several days to recover from the scourging alone. If he had been alive when taken down from the cross he would have been very weak and certainly would not have revived enough to be walking around so soon. The Jesus who was seen after the crucifixion was a resurrected Jesus, alive after death in a resurrected body, which was very similar to but not quite the same as his natural body and not much affected by the wounds. His resurrection body was not quite the same as his original body. It was visibly both the same and different.[15]

Secondly, if he had revived he was available to be rearrested and he never was. There were immediate problems for the authorities in Jerusalem when news of his appearances got out, and get out that news did – you never heard a rumour go round so fast. They will have hunted for him, high and low, all over the city and surrounding countryside. They didn't find him."

"Ummm!" said Gaius thinking hard, "I take your point. But is it possible there were two people involved? Either the man who died on the cross was not Jesus but someone who looked like him, and subsequently the real Jesus went around pretending that he had died and was resurrected, or Jesus did die on the cross and the person seen afterwards looked like him and pretended to be him." He looked hard at Jacob wondering how he would take these suggestions. They certainly seemed possible to him.

Jacob thought for a moment. "Yes, if Jesus had been an ordinary sort of person that might have happened. But he wasn't. You have not taken into account the personality of Jesus. It was his personality, not his physical appearance that was so different and made him unique. He might have been any village hill man, small and lithe and a strong easy walker. But his personality was extra-ordinary. He could dominate a crowd, even a very hostile crowd, easily, without raising his voice or appearing to do anything out of the ordinary. It is recorded that on one occasion he walked out through a lynch mob that was on the point of killing him.[16] Another time a crowd picked up stones to stone him and he just smiled and walked away – no one threw a single stone.[17] When a squad of soldiers were sent to arrest him they went all apologetic and really only took him into custody because he allowed them to do so.[18] He was hugely different.

How could two, nearly identical, men be found with personalities like that? It is impossible that there would be. It was his personality that was recognized after his resurrection. But his personality was overwhelmingly the same before and after his execution. He was simply unmistakable.

I haven't even pointed out that the people who were closest to him were the ones who recognized him. His mother, his cousin, his closest followers were all amongst those who saw him close to, both at his crucifixion and when he appeared afterwards.

Then there is the problem of his wounds – problem for

your theory, I mean. He specifically showed off his scars after his reappearance.[19] Whether that man was Jesus or the impostor how could he have been so badly scarred on his side, where the spear went into him, in his hands and feet where he was crucified and on his back where he was scourged? Making realistic scars would have been nearly as bad as the actual events the crucified man went through.

On at least two occasions he appeared in a closed and locked room.[20] One moment he was not there, the next he was. No one knew how he did it. They just had to accept the facts of what had happened. As I have already said, his resurrection body was subtly different from his natural body but yet he was always identified as the same man. His personality was overwhelmingly and obviously the same as it had been and so very different from everyone else's.

Also, of course, if there had been an ordinary person, one who had not been resurrected, walking around, whether Jesus or an impostor pretending to be Jesus, the authorities would certainly have arrested him and put him on display to stop the wild rumours, speculation and seething unrest that there was in Jerusalem in the days immediately after these events." Jacob paused for breath and then added with a twinkle in his eye, "Sorry, I talk too much, but I do think it is important to understand that what you suggest was just not possible."

Gaius raised both hands and dropped them again to show that he recognised that his argument did not succeed.

"I think I am beginning to run out of possible ways it could have happened," he said, "could this have been a mass hallucination, or could everybody have been hypnotised together?"

"No," said Jacob, "there is no such thing as a mass hallucination. Hallucinations are akin to dreams and therefore are individual. Nor can many people be hypnotised all at the same time like that, particularly in many different places, many miles apart, and at different times spread over a month. That is just not possible."

"Oh!" said Gaius, hesitating, and obviously lost to know what to say next.

Jacob went on, "There is one more possibility that you have not mentioned: that the disciples of Jesus made it all up. I have heard people trying to argue that that is what might have happened. I guess you did not want to say that because it would make it sound as though I was in on the deception and therefore a hypocrite to be sitting here talking like this."

Gaius smiled. "And I suppose since you mention it you must have a good answer to that one too!"

"Yes, I believe I have. Think for a moment. Here we are just 70 years after Jesus died. Have you heard of anywhere where there is not a group of believers in Jesus?"

"No, I haven't," said Gaius slowly. "You are going to go on to say that a faith which has spread so rapidly must be founded on truth."

"Yes, but there is even more to it than that. There are so many Christians now because of what the apostles, the twelve specially selected followers of Jesus, and all his other disciples, did after his death and resurrection. They immediately gave up their occupations; some of them left their homes and families and started to travel everywhere to tell people what had happened. Some went to Rome, others beyond Rome to Gaul,[21] some to Mesopotamia.[22] One, called Thomas, went east past Sirkap[23] in the valley of the Indus and on to the lands of the Tamils[24] far beyond the bounds of the Roman Empire. Others of them stayed at home, let it be known where they were and told many people what they had seen as eye-witnesses of what had happened. That was not a very safe thing to do either. I was one of these in a small way. Indeed talking to you like this I am still doing it!

Chapter 2

Also, I think I am right to say that of the original twelve men, or at least the eleven men who stayed with him, that Jesus chose as his special disciples, all but one died as a direct result of the work they undertook. Only one, called John, who died just five years ago, lived to die a natural death. Some of them died horrible deaths by crucifixion and other means of execution either at the hands of the authorities or at the hands of mobs. Would they have done that if they had known that the story they were telling was basically not true?"

"I suppose," said Gaius slowly, thinking hard, "people will die for a story that is not true if they do not know whether it is true or not. But they will not die for a story that they know for sure is false. I have to agree that that does not happen – or, does it? Will people not die for a story they know is false if they get sufficient benefit from it? No, I suppose they will live by a false story if it pays them well enough but they will try hard not to die for it. I am sorry, I am arguing with myself now."

"You are quite right," said Jacob with a smile, "but it has certainly been the case that this story did not pay well – as you put it – not in any earthly terms anyway. All these men lived in poverty; they travelled incessantly; they suffered many things before they died; it was not the sort of life anyone would choose to live unless they felt there was a very urgent and potent reason why they should do so."

Both men were quiet, saying nothing, as if by mutual agreement lost in their own thoughts. Several minutes passed and then Anna put her head round the corner of the doorway. "Would you like your supper now?" she asked, "It is all ready."

Jacob looked across to Gaius, who tried to look hungry. "Yes," he said, "we are both hungry, at least I am, and I am sure Gaius is after his long journey."

3

Gaius realised with a start that it had become almost completely dark, as they had been talking. Fortunately Anna had put some lamps in the room to which she now directed them.

They got up, Gaius again needing to help Jacob who was stiff from sitting still so long. Jacob led the way out of the courtyard into the room beyond the doorway. Gaius was glad to see a table loaded with good-looking food – meat dishes, freshly baked loaves, fruit and a jug of wine[25]. He was unsure whether he was expected to sit cross-legged on one of the platforms round the table or recline as a Roman or Greek would do on a formal occasion, so he watched to see what Jacob would do. Jacob eased himself down and sat cross-legged so Gaius was quick to move to the place Anna indicated for him and sit the same way himself. Anna sat at the foot of the table.

"We usually start our meals with a little ceremony," said Jacob. "Please forgive us if we do not include you since you are not a follower of Jesus. I think you will find what we do interesting, though."

Gaius was surprised, but quickly recovered himself, and said, "Of course, carry on."

Jacob took a round of unleavened bread, which looked exactly like a piece of naan or chapatti, held it up and tore it in two, saying "We take this bread and break it before you, Lord, in remembrance of your Son, our Saviour, Jesus. We eat it as a token of our fellowship in your sufferings, death and resurrection." He took a small piece from one half of the chapatti and ate it with his hands raised as though in prayer.

Then he passed the half chapatti to Anna who did

exactly the same. Returning it to the platter Jacob took a beaker from the table in front of him and lifted a jug, which was sitting in the middle of the table, and said, "We pour out this wine in remembrance of how your blood was poured out for us." He poured, what Gaius could see was red wine looking like blood, from the jug into the beaker. He replaced the jug on the table, lifted the cup and said "we drink from this cup as a token of our participation in your death and life."

He took a small sip of the wine and then passed the beaker to Anna who took a small sip too.

When he received it back Jacob put the cup on the table and said, "We ask you, Lord, to bless us and our friend as we talk together this night." Anna added, "To him who sits on the throne and to the Lamb be praise and honour, glory and power, for ever and ever!" Both Jacob and Anna then said "Amen!"

Jacob returned the broken chapatti to the plate with the rest of the bread and placed the beaker back in front of himself. He then filled it, and those in front of Gaius and Anna, pouring in first wine and then water.

He glanced across at Gaius who was looking very surprised and interested. "A very simple ceremony," he said with a smile, "a remarkably ordinary act of worship. But that is all that Jesus actually told us to do in remembrance of him. Nothing more.

In fact, we also do other things in worship: singing songs, reading from the ancient scriptures of Israel and the new writings we have about the life of Jesus, and other documents we think are special, encouraging each other and feasting together. But that is the simple act which is at the heart of our worship."

"Really?" asked Gaius, "I am very surprised. Do you have no priests or rabbis to lead worship? No sacrifices? No images to worship at? No ceremonial processions? Do you allow women to take an equal part in what you do?"

"We do have teachers," replied Jacob, "but none of the other things you mention. Women are human beings so they take a full part in everything we do." He said this with a slight grin wondering whether this would cause any reaction from Gaius. It didn't. "I know this is all very different from what is usually associated with a religion. But we need to be careful and not to go too fast! If I try to explain all those things now you will just get confused. Let's begin at the beginning, or at least continue from where we have got to."

Anna interrupted at this point to ask what they had been talking about while she was not with them. Between them Jacob and Gaius explained his questions and the answers that they had discussed so far. Anna turned to Gaius "Do you not believe in God?" she asked expressing by her tone of voice some surprise.

Gaius hesitated. "God!" He said, "Who is he? Do you mean the Jewish God? Or, one of the many gods of the Greeks and Romans? I find your question impossible to answer."

"No wonder," said Jacob. "I am glad to hear that you have realised that that question is difficult to answer. Sorry, Anna, but I think you have not thought that one through very well." Then, as Anna blushed, he added quickly, "I think we should start eating or the meat you have cooked so well will not be so nice. Let's take some food and start eating, then we can talk when we have taken the edge off our hunger."

Gaius was glad to hear that suggestion for he was very hungry. They passed the platters round and shared out the good food. There was silence for a few minutes as they all ate. When their rate of eating slowed down Anna could wait no longer. "Come on, Grandpa," she said, "I do want to hear what you are going to say in answer to that question

Chapter 3

'Who is God?' It is not something I have thought about at all. To me God has always just been, well, God. I've never stopped to think about him much, I'm afraid."

Jacob leant back, deep in thought. "Let me put it this way," he said. "The God that we know is completely and totally different from all the other gods people believe in. No other god I have ever heard about from any country is the least bit like the God we know and worship.

Two things in particular, are the distinguishing marks of our God, the true God. The first is that he is the Creator God. He created everything; everything is his handiwork. That is what Moses taught and it makes good sense. You will know that, Gaius, because that is how the Jewish scriptures start, 'In the beginning God created ...'[26]. The inevitable conclusion is that he has sovereign rights over all creation.

Secondly those Scriptures go on to say that God 'created man in his own image'[27]. That means man is able to be in relationship with God. God is not totally distant and completely other than man. There is the possibility of communication between God and man and even of concern and affection between them. Our ancient people understood that to be how they were to think of God. That is clear throughout the Scriptures: the Torah, the Psalms of David and the Writings of the prophets. Jesus told us that we are to take that idea one step further.

People used to think that God was the Father of Israel, the nation. Once the writer of a Psalm said that David would say God was his Father[28], meaning that was a very special and unusual thing to do. But Jesus taught that we as individuals may come to know that we can call God 'Father'. I think of God as my Father, just as Anna thinks of God as her Father. He is the Father of both of us as individuals. It is easy for us to forget how amazing that is. To call the Creator of the world 'Father', to be allowed and encouraged to do that, is just astonishing. It is almost unbelievable; but it is so."

He paused for a moment. It was Anna who broke the silence. "I never thought of it like that," she said slowly. "I suppose we get so used to calling God 'Father' we do forget the enormity of it."

"Yes. Of course, in a sense God is just God. We cannot describe him very accurately. We call him Father but he is far more than any earthly father is or ever could be. Even the best of earthly fathers are a pale reflection of what God is as Father."

There was another silence before Gaius spoke. "How do you know this is true," he asked. "You started off by talking about 'the God you know'. Shouldn't you have said 'the god you believe in' or 'the god that is your God'? To say you know him – well no one can say they know God. Particularly if he is the Creator of the world he must be so great and mysterious and far away he is far beyond the knowledge of any mere man. What you are talking about is not the way I was taught by my mother to understand God. For her God was very far away and very mysterious. To say that you know him is arrogant towards men and blasphemy towards God, isn't it?"

"It would be if we had not been asked and told to think of God in those ways," replied Jacob. "Let me quote you a few places in the Scriptures where this is very clear. Right back at the very beginning of the story of Abraham we read that God said:

"I will make of you a great nation, and I will bless you and make your name great, so that you will be a blessing. I will bless those who bless you, and him who dishonours you I will curse, and in you all the families of the earth shall be blessed."[29]

Those are not the words of a distant God but of a God who is prepared to bless those who honour him and worship him. Abraham was known as the friend of God.[30] You cannot be a friend of a remote and uninterested being.

It is recorded that, on one occasion, Abraham argued with God[31], asking him not to destroy the city of Sodom if there were righteous people in the city. First, he argued that the city should be saved for the sake of fifty people, then of forty-five, then forty, then thirty, twenty, finally of ten. You do not barter with God as though you are two merchants in the bazaar unless you are very confident in the love of God and his basic friendship towards you.

But above all we know that the descendants of Abraham have been blessed; their name has been made great; they are to this day a blessing to other peoples. Those promises made to Abraham have been richly fulfilled down through the years.

Then there is Jacob, the grandson of Abraham. He wrestled with God. Wrestled with one who could have destroyed him. What sort of God is it that descends to teach a man a lesson by wrestling with him?[32]

Moses stood in the presence of God and was not consumed. Instead we read that his face shone with the glory of God.[33] He too is called a friend of God.[34]

David, in his most famous Psalm, talks about God as his shepherd, his guide and his host at a banquet. He says, 'The LORD is my shepherd, ... I will fear no evil; for you are with me; ... You prepare a table before me in the presence of my enemies; you anoint my head with oil; my cup overflows.'[35]. All those images presume that God is approachable, that he is lovable, that he does love human beings, that he is both far away from us and prepared to be close to us."

He paused for breath and waited for a response from Gaius.

Gaius spoke slowly, obviously trying to find the words to express the new thoughts that were crowding into his mind.

"Yes, such a God is very different from the gods of the Greeks and Romans. They think their gods decide what they are going to do to human beings. They do not concern themselves with what those humans want or what they will feel or the effect of their actions as a god, or of the gods, upon them."

"But, as I said" Gaius's voice speeded up as he came back to more familiar thoughts; "this is not the God that my mother told me about either. At least it is not the way she thought God was like. Her God was a very distant person. She felt, even as she worshipped him, that he had given up on Israel that he did not care, that if he had cared he would have done something about the way in which the Romans controlled this land, that everything was wrong in the way her world was and that God was doing nothing about it. Why were her ideas about God so different from the God you have just been describing? I can remember hearing about the things you have mentioned concerning Abraham, Jacob, Moses and David. I know what you say is right. But that is not the way my mother, or the teachers in the synagogue, thought about God. Why was there so much difference?"

"That is difficult to say. I think it is because, in their hearts, men do not really want a God who is too close to them. It implies that he is interested in what they do and that is a very scary thought. Since he is a holy God it means that anyone who is going to be his friend needs to be holy too, or at least strive after holiness. Much better to keep him at arm's length, so to speak, have him only in heaven, far away. Much safer for us!

And one of the other strange things about God is that he wants men, and women, to be holy by behaving well to other people.

When he gave Moses the Ten Commandments on the mountain[36] only four of those basic commandments were about the way people were to behave towards God: no other gods, no idols, no blasphemy and keeping the Sabbath. All the other six were about how people are to treat each other. God said: honour parents, no murder, no adultery, no stealing, no false witness, no coveting.

Men, and women, don't like that. They want to be able to do what they want, except perhaps for remembering their God occasionally when they rush off to pray or to worship. It is much more convenient if your religion does not affect the way you live!

People say 'give us a set of rules about how we are to pray and worship and leave us to get on with our own lives'. That is what makes them happy. So from the beginning of time, and probably for ever afterwards, people are going to want nice rule based religions that don't affect the way people live too much. Life is much easier that way"

"Oh," said Gaius, "yes, that does make sense. That is what I see happening all round me." Then, after a pause for thought, he added, "but how do we know all this is true? That that it is the way things should be? That God really is like that?"

"The same way that we know about Jesus. We have the history of what happened. All the way from Adam, through Noah, Abraham, Moses, David, Isaiah we have the record of how God dealt with these people, how he took care of them, how he looked after them."

"May I say something," asked Anna, a little hesitantly.

"Yes, of course, my dear," said Jacob, while Gaius turned towards her curious to know what she wanted to add to such a philosophical discussion.

"I think there is another way we can know God and what he is like. When Johanan died," she turned to Gaius, "I was engaged to be married to him two years ago. He got caught up in a riot in Jerusalem and, although it was nothing to do with him and he was not involved, some Roman soldiers killed him." She turned back to Jacob, "I knew that God was with me in my grieving and sorrow. He was very real to me then and he was very close to me"

Gaius hesitated, both because he had had a similar experience himself and he was unsure what he could say that would not offend Anna. Eventually he only said, "How did that affect you? I mean, how did you know that God was with you? If you don't mind telling me."

"Not at all." She paused, frowning with the effort of describing her feelings, "I think my faith kept my mind straight and my emotions under control. Johanan was a follower of Jesus. He is now with Jesus in the immediate presence of the Lord God. That is a great comfort to me. Perhaps one day we shall meet again – I am not sure what exactly happens when we die. I know one day will be the day of resurrection when, like Jesus, we shall live again. We shall be overwhelmed by the immediate presence and glory of the Lord.

Also because of what Jesus taught us I was able to avoid having bitterness in my heart towards the soldiers who killed him.

What happens to us, even the worst things that happen to us, do not need to affect the emotions of our heart permanently. Of course they do affect us at first, but not forever, or at least not so deeply. What we think, what we feel, is more important than what happens to us. I am going to live the rest of my life remembering Johanan, but not endlessly grieving for him. I live in the Lord and with the Lord."

There was silence round the table for quite some time. Eventually Jacob broke it. "History, the story of other people and long ago, and the history of ourselves, me meeting the risen Jesus, and Anna here experiencing the comfort of the Lord in her sad bereavement, our stories, are what give us confidence in the God that we serve."

He stopped and Gaius asked another question, "You have just stopped talking about God and started talking about the Lord," he said, "at least, Anna started to talk about the Lord instead of about God. What does that mean? Are these the same names for the one God, or what?"

Jacob grinned and chuckled. "Well spotted, young man," he said. "Anna was not wrong, but that is an enormous subject and a very important one. Would you mind if we leave it until the morning? I am not as young as I used to be and I could do with my bed. I promise you we will explain that as soon as we get together again."

As they got up there was a commotion at the gate and a string of mules and donkeys came in with two cheerful young men leading them and following them. They hailed Jacob and Anna and greeted Gaius as well on their way through the courtyard to the back of the house.

"They are my brothers, Matthew and James" Anna explained. "They live in houses nearby but keep their animals here, in the stables round the back. They will be busy for quite some time so I will tell them about you when they have finished with their animals but you should not wait up to speak to them. I will make your excuses for you."

4

Gaius woke with a start and the immediate realization that it was quite late. The sun was strong on the wall of the room through the window. It took him a moment to remember where he was and what he was doing. When he did remember he smiled to himself, stretched, and rolled off the bed. After a moment's hesitation he remembered where the well and the toilet were and went out of his room to them. He splashed water in his face to wake himself up more thoroughly, scrubbed his teeth with one of the small sticks lying on a shelf beside the well and pulled his rather crumpled tunic straight.

Then, a little hesitantly, he went to the room where they had eaten last night. He saw some porridge in a basin, bread, honey and a jug of water on the table. There was no one in sight. But he was still hungry after his long walk. So he had no difficulty deciding that it would be all right to help himself to some porridge, a lump of bread and a piece of honey comb dripping with honey.

The porridge disappeared very rapidly and he was getting himself thoroughly sticky with honey when he was aware of a movement in the room and saw that Anna had put her head round the corner of the door and was regarding him with some amusement. He tried to say "good morning" but it came out as a rather embarrassed mumble through the bread and honey. Anna was laughing outright as she returned his greeting.

"You are a sleepy head," she said. "My brothers have been and gone. We have just finished our morning prayers and worship, so my grandpa will be along in a minute."

Gaius felt apologetic. "I'm not really used to walking so far," he said. He also expressed his surprise. "So that was another act of informal worship without a priest," he went on, more as a statement than a question. He was beginning to get used to the strange ways of the Christians. "And did you take part in that too?" he asked.

"Yes, of course," was the smiling reply. "We have a leader of the church when we worship, who is grandfather Jacob, and under his control all of us who have set out to follow Jesus are free to take part. We are all equal before the Lord.

The apostle Paul, who did so much to build up the churches, said about us, 'in Christ Jesus you are all sons of God through faith ... there is neither Jew nor Greek, there is neither slave nor free, there is neither male nor female, for you are all one in Christ Jesus. And if you are Christ's, then you are Abraham's offspring, heirs according to promise.'"[37]

Gaius was quick to respond. "Who are the 'you' of that statement? Abraham's offspring? Doesn't it mean just Jews[38] who follow Jesus?"

"No, of course not. Paul said 'neither Jew nor Greek' and that statement was made in a letter he wrote to a group of Christians living a long way north of here, much further from the Jewish lands. Most of them were not Jews at all but ordinary people living in the province of Galatia."

"But then how can they be described as Abraham's seed as they were in that statement? It doesn't make sense."

"Yes, it does! Paul was saying that it is not natural descent from Abraham that is important but having the same sort of faith and trust in his God as he had. The promise to Abraham was that 'in you all the families on earth shall be blessed.' All families, all peoples! We are the fulfilment of that great promise. Whoever we are. Of whatever tribe or clan. Wherever we live. Whatever our status in life – slave or free. Man or woman. Provided we have come to accept that Jesus is our Saviour and Lord."

It was only when she paused for breath that Gaius could

get a word in. "But what you say still does not make sense," he argued back. "You talk about having the same faith in his God, Abraham's God, as he had. But that is not what we have been talking about. You have been talking about having faith in Jesus. Jesus was not Abraham's God. You can't equate the two, the two gods. They are different."

"Which is exactly the same point we finished on last night when you asked who we meant when we talked about 'the Lord'" came a voice from behind Gaius. "Good morning, young man. I hear that you are having a good time with my argumentative young granddaughter!" Both Gaius and Anna broke into broad grins as they turned to Jacob.

"Well, yes," admitted Gaius. "I think we were both enjoying ourselves." Anna blushed slightly, but couldn't help grinning even more broadly.

"Please, if you are going to discuss the answer to that question, can I sit with you and hear the discussion?" she asked.

"And take part in it, I have no doubt," replied Jacob. "Yes, of course," then, turning to Gaius "that is if you do not mind."

"Not at all," said Gaius, with a smile and delight in his heart that such a lovely and interesting girl should be prepared to think about such things and argue about them.

"Come on then," said Jacob, further surprising Gaius by starting to clear the table, which was not something he was used to men doing, particularly older men. Anna quickly moved to help him. "Put those things through the back and then come on through. We will wait for you before we start."

Jacob moved slowly. He walked through to the seat he had the previous day and sat himself down comfortably. Gaius excused himself, dashed through to rinse his hands at the well, and returned to sit down beside him. By then Anna had come swiftly through and found herself a cushion to sit on beside them.

Chapter 4

Jacob began. "Who exactly was Jesus? That question has puzzled everybody from the very beginning. Even his earliest disciples were not sure at first. In fact they got it wrong for quite a while. They accepted that he was the long promised Messiah, the Anointed One that the prophets of the Scriptures said would come. They thought that meant he was going to be the great leader who would liberate the land from the Romans, turn the usurping kings of the Herodian family out of power and establish the direct rule of the God of Abraham, Isaac and Jacob over his own people and his own land. Judaea would once again stand proud and free amongst the nations. God would be honoured because of them and their power.

But they slowly realized that - if Jesus was the Messiah - he was not at all the sort of Messiah they were thinking about. He was the very opposite of the sort of war leader that would be necessary to do those things. Just before his death Jesus said, 'My kingdom is not of this world. If my kingdom were of this world, my servants would have been fighting, that I might not be delivered over to the Jews. But my kingdom is not from the world.'[39]

I can probably explain that best by quoting to you two statements made by the greatest of all the prophets, Isaiah, many hundreds of years ago. He said, speaking prophetically about the Messiah:

'Behold my servant, whom I uphold,
my chosen, in whom my soul delights;
I have put my Spirit upon him;
he will bring forth justice to the nations.
He will not cry aloud or lift up his voice,
or make it heard in the street;
a bruised reed he will not break,
and a faintly burning wick he will not quench;
he will faithfully bring forth justice.
He will not grow faint or be discouraged

till he has established justice in the earth;

and the coastlands wait for his law.'[40]

He also said, again speaking prophetically as if he was the Messiah himself:

'The Spirit of the Lord God is upon me,

because the Lord has anointed me

to bring good news to the poor;

he has sent me to bind up the broken-hearted,

to proclaim liberty to the captives,

and the opening of the prison to those who are bound;

to proclaim the year of the Lord's favour.'[41]

And when Jesus read that passage out in the synagogue in Nazareth he added: 'Today this scripture has been fulfilled in your hearing.'[42]

In those two passages what sort of person was the prophet expecting, do you think?"

Gaius and Anna looked at each other to see who would answer first. Gaius took the lead. "I see what you mean when you say it was not a war leader Isaiah was looking for. He thought the Messiah would be a quiet and peaceful man. But he also seems to have expected this man to bring justice to the whole world. I don't see how any man could do that. You can't be peaceful and bring justice to the world. The two things just don't go together. You have to have an army to bring peace. We have had peace here, more or less, these last 30 years because of the Roman army."

Anna broke into the discussion in a soft and puzzled voice, "you mean you have to fight to bring peace!"

Gaius stopped and hesitated. "It sounds stupid doesn't it? 'Fight for peace' makes a poor slogan, I suppose. But isn't that just the way things are? What other way is there?"

"None, if you treat men that way," agreed Jacob. "But suppose you can give men the desire within themselves to want peace and justice. Isn't it possible for them to have both things? Persuading men to want peace and justice is much more effective than telling them they should be peaceful and just. If you just tell them that, you have to back up your command, for that is what it would be, with an army.

And what about the second quotation I gave you? The Messiah that Isaiah foresaw was to be a preacher of good news, a healer of broken hearts, a releaser of prisoners and one who would free those captive to others and to their own selves. Jesus taught about this other way; a way of peace and quiet hearts. A way of love in which every man and every woman will be kind and good to their neighbour and even their enemy. We have Roman soldiers from the encampment at the next village who have become followers of Jesus coming across to worship with us and we get on very well with them. They are learning to be good and kind men even while they are true to their oath of allegiance as soldiers of the Roman Empire. They prove that the two things, peace and justice, can go together."

"Yes," said Anna. She continued, hesitantly and with a shy look across to her grandfather, "I was at the other end of the village a few months ago when two soldiers stopped me and started talking to me in a quite aggressive and unpleasant way. But then another soldier, I had never seen before, saw what they were doing and came over and stopped them. I thought there was going to be a fight; two against one, but the two ruffians were obviously in awe of the third man although he was just an ordinary soldier. He was very kind to me and brought me across the village, telling me about his family as we walked to put me at my ease. Then, at our very next meeting, he came in with Apelles."

Jacob looked at her in obvious amazement. "You never told me that before," he said. "Was that it, then? I wondered why you greeted a Roman I had not seen before as though you knew who he was and smiled on him so much. What happened to him? I don't remember seeing him again."

"Yes, Grandpa. I didn't tell you because I didn't want to upset you, or mother. I would have asked him to the house but he was posted out of the camp the next week and we never saw him again. But it was good to have met him and recognized that what he did was part of his faithfulness to the way of Jesus."

"The things young people don't tell you nowadays!" Jacob commented, "Yes, that is a good example of the way of peace – even if the man had to threaten to fight to defend Anna!"

They all laughed.

"Isaiah prophesied about a mysterious man that he called the servant, the servant of God. He said he would be 'despised and rejected by men, a man of sorrows, and acquainted with grief.[43]' And that is exactly who Jesus was. He fulfilled that prophecy from several hundred years earlier."

"Ummm!" said Gaius thinking hard, "but how does Jesus being a servant tie in with the way in which you people worship him as though he is a god?"

"You have made a huge assumption there," retorted Jacob. "Why do you think that being a servant and being God are incompatible? Remember what we talked about last night when we agreed - at least I thought we did - that God might not be quite the way we tend to think of him.

You are bringing into your vision of what God is like certain ideas that are very different from the ideas about God that were implicit in what Jesus said and did.

You are not to be blamed. Everybody else tends to make exactly the same mistake. It was only when we started to look back at the Scriptures, after Jesus died and was resurrected, at what Moses, David and the prophets had said, that we realized that those ideas Jesus had talked about had been there all the time and we had been blind to them.

Chapter 4

We were so carried away with ideas about the otherness of God, that he could not be approached by human beings, that he is remote and distant and full of wrath and judgment, that we did not see how close he is to us. Remember how I said yesterday that he made us in his own image and likeness; he spoke face to face with Abraham and Moses; he loved his people; he put up with all sorts of infidelities on their part; he saved them, comforted them and protected them even when they did not deserve it.

He had a love and concern for all the world. He intended that all the world should be blessed through his people and it was only when they proved completely incompetent at that task that he sent Jesus to do what they had failed to do.

Let me ask you a question now: Where do you get your vision of what God is like from?"

"That is an interesting question," said Gaius thoughtfully "with no easy answer. I suppose I would have to admit that it is a mixture of what my mother taught me and what the teachers in the synagogue said, all mixed in with something of how my pagan friends think about god or the gods. Their gods are all very different from human beings, worse than humans in many ways in fact. But as you say their main idea is that they are far away, remote and unconcerned about human beings. Indeed, that it is impossible to understand what they do; that their decisions are beyond human understanding; even that they change their minds and are not responsive to any principles of justice or fairness. I suppose we tend to take those ideas and think that the one true God must be just the same. At least that is what I have done.

So when you put all that together I think of God as majestic and awe-inspiring, remote, distant and unconcerned about me. He, God, or they, gods, decide what will happen on earth, but they do not take any account of me when they make those decisions. I just have to put up with what happens. Just possibly I can persuade them to do things differently and in a way that is better for me if I pray to them, give money to their holy people or make sacrifices to them. But it is all very doubtful whether it is any good, whether it actually works."

Jacob turned to Anna. "What is your vision of God?" he asked her.

"Quite different," she replied. "I suppose it is the result of being brought up in a Christian household. I do not think of God in anything like the way Gaius describes. To me he is kind and helpful – a bit like you grandpa, though much grander and more awe-inspiring. But I like him, indeed, I would say that I love him."

"That is good, my dear. But I am glad you called him awe-inspiring. It is too easy for Christian young people to start to think of God in too light a way and make him into just a pleasant old man who will do them no harm. Thinking of him as being too close to us is every bit as much a distortion as erring in the other direction of having him too far away. The God we believe in is both near to us, in our very hearts and lives, and at the same time far away in all the splendour of his heavenly realm. That is the way he described himself to Moses when he said he was:

"The Lord, the Lord, a God merciful and gracious, slow to anger, and abounding in steadfast love and faithfulness, keeping steadfast love for thousands, forgiving iniquity and transgression and sin, but who will by no means clear the guilty, visiting the iniquity of the fathers on the children and the children's children, to the third and the fourth generation.[44]"

"But what does this have to do with Jesus?" asked Gaius. "Where does he stand in relation to God? I have been told that Christians worship Jesus as if he was God, or is God. So you have got two gods, unlike the Jews who are very careful to say that they have only one God.

They have been, and are being, persecuted because they refuse to worship anybody else's god; in particular, because they refuse to worship Caesar as a god. You won't have the same trouble because if you worship two gods you must be prepared to worship other gods as well. Won't you...." He paused noticing the frown on Jacob's face and wondering whether he had said too much.

"Hear, O Israel: The Lord our God, the Lord is one. You shall love the Lord your God with all your heart and with all your soul and with all your might.[45]" Jacob said slowly. "You will know that?"

"The Shema. The great statement of the oneness of God that every faithful Jew recites twice every day. But I don't see how that answers my question. There is no doubt that the Jews worship only one God. But what about the Christians?"

"Let me explain it by quoting something the apostle Paul said. He brought the good news about Jesus to many places throughout the world many years ago. He wrote a letter to the Christians gathering in the city of Corinth. In it he said this: 'for us there is one God, the Father, from whom are all things and for whom we exist, and one Lord, Jesus Christ, through whom are all things and through whom we exist.'[46]

If we take out the two descriptions he said simply 'there is one God, the Father; and one Lord, Jesus Christ.'

Do you see? In it he carefully split up the Shema so that the one God is God the Father and the one Lord is the Lord Jesus Christ. He was saying that when we talk about God we include Jesus in God. He was God, specifically the God of Abraham, Isaac and Jacob, walking on earth."

"But that doesn't help," retorted Gaius. "God is god. There is no room in him for a man. Paul could split up the Shema but that does not make it right. You cannot sneak Jesus in to your definition of God like that and still claim to believe in one God."

"Don't be so sure about that," replied Jacob. "The people of God always knew that there was only one God but they did not limit him in the way you are trying to do. What I am hoping to make you understand is that if Paul, a brilliant man, very learned in the Hebrew Scriptures and the Jewish faith and totally convinced that God is one, could include Jesus in his statement about God, we should do so too. What do we put first: our ideas of what God is like or what he has told us he is like?"

"Ummm!" said Gaius thoughtfully.

He said no more so Jacob continued, "There is an interesting story about Abraham in the Torah of Moses. God visited Abraham to speak to him. It is described like this: 'And the Lord appeared to him by the oaks of Mamre, as he sat at the door of his tent in the heat of the day. He lifted up his eyes and looked, and behold, three men were standing in front of him. When he saw them, he ran from the tent door to meet them... And Abraham went quickly into the tent to Sarah and said, 'Quick! Get some fine flour! Knead it, and make cakes.'' Then it says 'the men set out from there, and they looked down toward Sodom. And Abraham went with them to set them on their way. The Lord said, "Shall I hide from Abraham what I am about to do

And the Lord went his way, when he had finished speaking to Abraham, and Abraham returned to his place. The two angels came to Sodom in the evening, and Lot was sitting in the gate of Sodom. When Lot saw them, he rose to meet them and bowed himself with his face to the earth and said, "My lords, please turn aside to your servant's house....""[47]

Who did Abraham meet? Two men, three men, three angels, the LORD, or what?"

"I know that story," said Anna, leaning forward in her keenness to understand what her grandfather was saying.

"I think we are meant to understand that there were two angels with a man who was the Lord. They all looked like men, and sat down and ate a meal like men, but not all was what it seemed to be."

"Which does not fit in with a neat and tidy picture of God being one and only, and all alone, and quite different from us," added Gaius. "My point exactly," said Jacob, pleased that his two students were understanding him so well. "The God in whom we believe is one. I am, of course, talking about the God in whom all the children of Abraham believe, whose special personal name is YAHWEH. When we say 'he is one' that is a statement about the identity of God and not a statement of numerical calculation. All the prophets from Moses talked about the Spirit of God, the Word of God, the Glory of God, the Name of God and the Wisdom of God, all of them as God, without implying that there was anything other than one God. So, for instance, we are told that at the creation the 'Spirit of God was hovering over the waters'[48] and also that Wisdom was there for Wisdom says 'when he marked out the foundations of the earth, then I was beside him like a master workman.[49]' Given that sort of statement, talking about Jesus as God in phrases like "Grace and peace from God the Father and Christ Jesus our Saviour"[50] are not so surprising as you think. The early disciples simply worshipped Jesus as God because that was what they considered him to be, and they did not get hung up in arguments about how God could be one and three at the same time."

"What about the third of the three?" asked Gaius, "Where does that come in?"

"The third is the Spirit, the Spirit of God or the Holy Spirit. One of the last things Jesus taught his disciples was that after his death they would receive help from "another Helper or Counsellor"[51] who would be the Spirit of truth. They did get that help. He arrived visibly, first on a special day, fifty days after the resurrection of Jesus. We have discovered that we too have had the Holy Spirit active in our lives ever since. Because Jesus said the Counsellor would replace himself and would have the same status that he had, once Jesus was acknowledged as God, so was the Counsellor.

But I think we should stay with our subject of who Jesus was and leave the question of the Holy Spirit until later."

"At this rate," said Gaius with a grin, "we shall never be finished because we are generating more questions than we are answering!"

"True," agreed Jacob, "but you did say you wanted them all answered!"

"Coming back to the question of Jesus," said Anna thoughtfully, "who did Jesus think that he was? What did he actually say about himself? Did he ever actually say that he was God?"

"That is a very good question," said Jacob. "The answer has to be 'yes' and 'no'. No. He never said 'I am God'. But also - Yes. He actually said something even more powerful. To say that he was god, that he was divine, would not have meant very much in our world of many so-called gods. He did not say that he was God but he did say that he was YAHWEH, the God of Abraham, Isaac and Jacob."

"I've never heard that before," replied Anna with a puzzled frown. "Go on."

"Jesus had to be very careful. If he had not been he would have been killed earlier than he was in a riot in some remote Jewish village and not in Jerusalem before the world, as he eventually had to be.

When Moses asked God at the burning bush what his name was he got three answers of which the most important was a simple statement of existence: 'I AM' in Hebrew, which, in Greek, is also "I AM" or just 'I am.'[52] Then when God spoke through the great prophet Isaiah he said 'I

AM God. Also henceforth I am he.'[53]

Jesus used that very same phrase 'I AM' to refer to himself. Of course, that phrase is also a perfectly ordinary one that simply says 'It's me!' or 'Here I am!'. When Jesus used it he did so very carefully so that most times those who heard him were not sure whether he was just saying 'It's me' or using that phrase to mean he was God. So on one occasion he called to his disciples, who were not sure whether the person they were seeing in the dark was him or not 'I am; do not be afraid'[54] using exactly those words which are the name of God. They did not know for sure whether he meant the simple meaning or was making the very deep claim to be YAHWEH. But another time when he said it those who heard were quite sure he was saying he was YAHWEH. He said 'I tell you the truth, before Abraham was, I AM!'[55] in Hebrew using exactly those words. That time he nearly got himself killed because some of those listening to him picked up stones to stone him, and he had to slip away and hide himself.[56]

So in that rather clever way he did say that he was YAHWEH, the LORD the prophets spoke about, but only so that those who were listening very carefully heard him say it."

"Phew! That is hard to follow," said Anna. "But I think I understand. Jesus said that he was YAHWEH, and therefore God and the Lord. I am happy to accept that. What I don't understand is how he could be God and then talk about God as his Father and himself as the Son of God. If he was God that must mean that all of God was in him. But if he distinguishes between himself and the Father doesn't that mean that not all of God was in him. They are two distinct persons, or Gods, or something?"

"Yes. It is difficult," agreed Jacob. "But that seems to be the way it is. I know thoughtful people have a problem with how Jesus could be God and God still be one. I just think we must not let our logic determine what we think about God. If he tells us, as I believe he has, that he is God the Father and Jesus is God the Son then that is fine by me. I have to accept that."

"Do you mean that God had intercourse with Jesus' mother and they had a son together?" asked Gaius, his voice bearing a distinct note of surprise at his own thought.

"Good gracious, no!" burst out Jacob sounding very startled at that suggestion. "Of course not!" But then he quietened down and continued "Sorry! I was taken aback by what you said but I suppose it is a reasonable thing to think if you hear the phrase 'son of god'. I know the Caesars think they become gods when they die. So every Caesar who is Caesar because he is the son of a Caesar thinks he is a son of a god. Augustus Caesar called himself the son of the divine Julius Caesar. Jesus' birth was strange but not in that way. What the prophets meant when they spoke about the sons of God was quite different. The kings of Israel used to be called the sons of God. Sometimes God called the whole nation of Israel his son. It is a statement about status not about physical generation."

"You mean it was a title like Prince or King?"

"Yes, those are good examples of an equivalent."

"But there is still a problem," continued Gaius with a puzzled frown. "If God did not have intercourse with Jesus' mother, who did? How could he be so special and be called the Son of God if he was only the child of his human father? Surely there is a problem there?"

"Yes, there is! And the answer is strange, I must admit. The mother of Jesus was a virgin when he was born! The power of God overshadowed her and she had a child – but she was a virgin who had never lain with a man!"

"Good gracious!" retorted Gaius. "That must have caused a mighty stir in the village. Did people believe her when she said she was a virgin?"

"Not all of them! Not many of them! But that is the unvarying testimony of those who should know. And it does fit in with everything else that happened at the time of his birth and afterwards. It is strange but I do believe that is what actually happened."

There was a pause as Gaius tried to absorb this startling information. Eventually he shrugged his shoulders. "I have to accept your testimony," he said finally, and a bit reluctantly.

Jacob was clearly relieved when Gaius said that. "There have been some really hard questions there. I hope my answers are satisfactory even if they are not easy to understand. I think we should move on to discuss something else, but, before we do that, I would like to show you something that may help. It is to illustrate how we should think about God and Jesus. It is not a perfect picture – nothing in this world ever can be, I suppose, because we are trying to explain the mystery of the person of God in human words and ideas. But it may help.

Anna, my dear, please fetch through that big wooden plate you use for putting the bread on and your bags of lentils. I want three different colours of lentils. I think you will have those, don't you?"

Anna got up quickly. "Yes, grandpa. We have red, yellow and black lentils. I'll get them."

She disappeared in a hurry and reappeared very quickly with the large wooden plate and three small bags. Jacob took the plate from her and placed it on the ground. He put his hand into the first bag and took out a small handful of lentils, only about 12 of them, in fact. He carefully placed them in a small pile at one side of the plate. Then he took lentils of another colour and made another separate pile another side of the plate. Finally the third colour of lentils made a third small pile. Gaius and Anna watched, in some puzzlement as to what he was doing.

"There," said Jacob. "How many piles of lentils are there on that plate?"

"Three," said Anna. Jacob picked up the plate and with one quick shake of his wrist shot all the lentils down to one side of the platter.

"How many piles did you say there are?" asked Jacob expressing puzzlement in his tone of voice.

"One," said Gaius.

"But if you give me a moment," said Jacob, "you will see that there are three!" starting to sort out the lentils as he spoke.

Anna chuckled. "All right, Grandpa, you don't need to sort them all out. I will do that later. We get your point. One, or three. Who knows?"

"As I said it is not a perfect illustration. It would be easy to criticize it. The lentils should be unique, more special than any other on earth. But it might help you to see how God can be one but include Jesus and the Holy Spirit with the Father."

"That has been a long hard discussion," said Anna. "But it is great fun. I love trying to think through these things. Let's have something to eat and to drink before we start on the next subject – what is it going to be anyway, Grandpa?"

"Well! It's easy to get so stuck on the question of how Jesus could be God that we miss the much more important questions of why he was God; and why, if he was God, did he die. If he was God, could he die? What was it all about?"

5

After a hard morning's discussion they had a slow and leisurely lunch. While Anna was preparing it Gaius spent his time thinking about all the things they had talked about. He wrestled with the problem of changing his ideas about God to those that Jacob had suggested. He had not thought very much about the Messiah. He knew many of the more traditional people had thought he would appear sometime in the future and carry his people to independence and victory by the strength of his leadership and his ability as a war commander. It was rather difficult to think of the Messiah as the exact opposite, a man of peace. He found it very difficult to see how the Messiah could also be God because that would mean that God was a God of peacefulness and quiet, quite unlike the God he had been brought up to believe in.

During lunch they carefully avoided the subject of their discussions although they had made no agreement to do so. They talked about many things – the state of the country, the situation with the Roman occupation, the latest rumours of what the insurgents were likely to do next, the anticipated good harvest and many other things they were all interested in. Then Gaius had to explain who he was and how and why he was in their area. That took some time.

Finally the meal was cleared away; Jacob had finished the short sleep he liked to take after lunch; Anna had finished her work in the kitchen; Gaius, who had been thinking hard, was as full of questions as ever.

"You suggested that we should think about why Jesus died," he said to start the discussion.

"Yes," said Jacob. Gaius missed the slight twinkle in his eyes as he started his reply. "This is something that has been argued about ever since it happened. Some say that it was all because of the leaders in Jerusalem. They were furious about the way Jesus was leading the crowds to think in a totally different way from the one that was traditional amongst them. They could see that the power they exercised, the status they had as teachers of the Law, and the income they derived from these things would all be much reduced, or lost altogether, if the teaching of Jesus became widely accepted.

Others say it was all done by the Romans. They were in charge of the country and were the only people who could legally apply the death penalty. They wanted the country to stay peaceful and did not much care who the people followed so long as the peace was kept and they and Caesar were properly respected.

I think both were equally responsible and guilty for what was done to Jesus. Since the Jews were the religious authorities and the Romans were the ruling authority they represented all people and we were all in some measure responsible. They did what we would have done if we had been in their places ...."

Gaius interrupted. "Excuse me," he said, "that isn't really what I was interested in. I must have put my question badly. What I was thinking about was why did Jesus die if he was God? How could God die? What possible reason could there be for him allowing himself to be killed if indeed he was God? Surely the one sure thing about God is that he cannot die; he will not die; he cannot be killed by men? Was God not in control?"

He was surprised by Jacob's reaction. "Well done, young man," he said. "You are beginning to think the right thoughts. Perhaps I was being a bit unfair. I started talking about the details of the human reasons why Jesus was executed just to see if you realized there are far more difficult and important questions behind what happened.

You have clearly seen that there are. Let me ask you a question: if Jesus was God why would he allow himself to be killed? Would he allow that to happen without a purpose?"

"No. I don't think so," replied Gaius. "He must have had some very good reason to die. Though what it could be I cannot begin to imagine. You will have to explain it very carefully!"

"Jesus died to gain the greatest victory of all time," Jacob began to say.

That was such a surprising statement Gaius broke in immediately. "But how can his death at the hands of common Roman soldiers possibly be a victory," he asked.

"What is a victory?" responded Jacob and answered his own question, "A victory is when someone emerges from a battle having gained the things that they want to gain. We always think of victory in terms of gaining strength and power, gaining dominance, gaining control over the enemy. But if you are a person who thinks the best things in life for which we should all strive are love, peace, truthfulness, modesty, then victory takes on a different aspect all together. Jesus had clearly taught a different way from that of the world. I like to think of it as 'the way up is down'. By the standards of Caesar, the army commander, the ruler of the region, and the ordinary citizen, power and strength are up, so love and peace must be down. Jesus taught that is exactly the wrong way round. 'The way up is down'. What happens when we apply that line of thought to the death of Jesus?"

There was a long pause as Gaius and Anna tried to think out the implications of what Jacob had just said. Eventually Anna spoke up. "You mean that Jesus behaved in the way that he said was good and right even when that led directly to his death. He went what we would call down to degradation and death, but he considered that to be the way up because in dying he was showing his love. He was willing to appear to be weak, to be over powered, to be dominated, to be controlled because, to him, strength, power, domination and control are not the great things of life."

"Wow!" was all that Gaius could think of to say. There was a long silence. "Does that mean God is like that?"

Jacob nodded. "I think you have seen the point of what happened.

But there is more to it than that. Jesus did not die only to establish his way over the way of the world. Evil may be the evil of a religion that enslaves people spiritually, or of a government that dominates people economically and socially, or even just the actions of people who lust for power and don't care who they hurt in getting it. That is the way of the world. Jesus certainly wanted to defeat those sorts of evil. But there is even more to it than that. And it is here that we see the thing that really affects us all as individuals. Jesus died to defeat sin and its consequences in you and me."

"I see," said Anna slowly.

"I don't," retorted Gaius. "What do you mean by sin? My teachers told me that I should obey the law: keep the Sabbath, obey the food laws, and keep all the Torah so far as I know it. Not doing so was what they called sin. I never could understand them. It all seemed so well designed to further their influence and power. I cannot see that it has much, or anything, to do with God – particularly, come to think of it, if he is anything like you have described."

"It is good to talk to someone who thinks things out the way you do, Gaius," said Jacob with a slow smile growing across his face.

He continued, "You are quite right. Sin, as Jesus taught about it, is very little to do with keeping the many detailed laws of religious observance. Jesus simply ignored most of

Chapter 5

those laws, but went into considerable and alarming detail about the laws that really matter, the ones about the way we behave and what we are deep inside.

He said that we break the law of murder if we are angry with our brother – or our sister[57]. I think he said that because he wanted us to understand that anger comes from the same attitude inside our minds and hearts as murder does. The anger that makes someone commit murder is a great deal worse than the anger that makes someone shout at people in their own family and that in turn is worse than being angry and bottling it up inside you. But God knows that in all three cases the person has turned away from his way of love in his or her heart. Any turning away from God and his ways is sin which brings us into judgment."

"Umm." Gaius grunted and thought for a moment. "If that is true - and it does make good sense - in spite of everything, we all fall under judgment. We all get angry sometimes."

"Yes, indeed. Jesus went on to say that anyone who looks on a woman to lust commits adultery with her in his heart[58]."

"Does that mean I cannot even look at a woman? That seems ridiculous!" said Gaius with a sideways glance at Anna who grinned back at him mischievously.

"No, of course not," replied Jacob. "I know some religious people say women should always be covered up so that men are not tempted to lust when they see them. Jesus was much more realistic about who we are and had a far higher view than that of what human beings are capable of. He clearly wanted each man to control his own thoughts and actions and each woman too. He was interested in what we are inside, the way we think, what our motives are, not just what we do and what we look like to the outside world. We are responsible for both what we do and who we are. We have powers of choice and of decision. Ultimately it is what we are inside that determines what we do. However hard we try we cannot be one thing inside and another thing outside. Inside badness will eventually show in wrong actions."

Anna spoke up at that. "I heard someone in the church, who I know had done something completely stupid and had a bad accident as a result – I had better not say who it was – say that what had happened to him was inevitable because God is in control and we could not do anything that was against the will of God. He seemed to think he had no choice in the matter. He had to do the stupid thing. Are you saying that he was completely wrong? That he did have a choice and what he did would show what he was really like inside? And it would not depend on what God made him do?"

"Yes, I am," said Jacob. "God is all powerful and he does rule the world. But we are not to assume that because he ultimately determines everything that happens we do not have to make wise and proper decisions all the time. If you wander in front of a galloping horse you will get knocked down and it will be your fault. We are human beings, not animals, and we alone have been given the power of foresight and the ability to plan ahead and be responsible for our decisions.

But we are not sticking to our main subject – why did Jesus die.

We are all sinful and when we come into judgment before the throne of God in the last day we will all be found guilty. We will all be rejected and not allowed into the eternal kingdom. It doesn't matter how well we are born or what our family is. It doesn't matter what race or people we belong to. It doesn't matter how well we behave, either in matters of religious observance or in our dealings with our fellow men and women. We are not good enough, not one of us is good enough, to stand before the throne of the perfect and holy God and be accepted on the Day of Judgment. To believe that God will overlook our sinfulness because we have done this or that good work or been properly religious is to have a God who is too small and too weak to be any good to anyone!"

He paused, and looked across to Gaius to see what his reaction would be.

Gaius grunted and looked unhappy. "I have to accept what you say," he said, rather slowly. "It makes good sense." He stopped. The others waited as he was clearly going to say something else. "If I am honest I have to admit that I had actually thought that out for myself, some time ago, but it was such an unwelcome thought I have been careful to try and forget it." Another pause for thought followed. "But what has that got to do with the death of Jesus? Why does his death have any effect at all on me?"

Jacob took a deep breath and replied, "I am going to tell you a story. You will already know the details of it but you may not have seen what it all means. Settle yourself comfortably for it is quite a long story!

As I said yesterday God created Adam and Eve. We are told that he 'created man in his own image, in the image of God he created him; male and female he created them.'[59] I think that being 'created in the image of God' refers to the fact that he breathed spirit into them. They became by that act special and very different from any animal. They became able to relate to God and to each other in a different way.

He gave them only one simple commandment: that they should not eat of the tree of the knowledge of good and evil; but they disobeyed and ate.[60] Eve ate first but Adam was at fault as well. They were in it together and equally guilty. Sin – disobedience to the express command of God – had come into the world. From that first sin the principle of sin grew through the human race like a cancer. Their son Cain killed his brother Abel.[61] Before long the whole world was so evil that only Noah and his family were saved from the flood.[62] Then the arrogance of men was such that they built the tower of Babel[63] to try to control the earth and everything in it.[64] It was all bad news about men and women."

"May I interrupt," asked Gaius.

"Yes, of course."

"Are you saying that all men and women are bad all the time?"

"No, I am not. What I am saying is that we are all made in the image of God but we have all sinned so our potential has been spoiled and we are all sinners. That is what the Bible teaches us and that is how we find the world we live in to be. To take the extremes: there are brutal brigands who live by killing, and look after their own children with great care and tenderness and there are pleasant, mild shopkeepers in the market who beat their wives for no reason at all when they get home. We are all strange mixtures of good and bad. The division between good and evil does not run between us humans dividing between good people and bad people; it runs right through the middle of each one of us.

That is the only sensible way to look at human beings. Some people try to argue that each one of us is basically all good and the bad that we unfortunately do some times doesn't really matter too much. There are others who say we are all bad and overlook the good things that we do. Neither is true to what we can see going on all around us. We all know that most of our neighbours are nice people whether they have ever heard of the Lord or not. We also know that they are far from perfect people – just like us!"

Gaius smiled. "Alright, I concede the point. I suppose it really is the only sensible way to understand people, far better than all the things the Greek philosophers tried to teach us in the schools I went to. Go on."

"God had a plan. He chose Abraham to be the man, and have the family who would put the world of men to rights. I have already quoted to you what he said to Abraham. Here it is again:

'I will make of you a great nation, and I will bless you and make your name great, so that you will be a blessing. I will bless those who bless you, and him who dishonours you I will curse, and in you all the families of the earth shall be blessed'[65]

But Abraham's descendants did not follow the Lord with all their hearts by obeying him as he asked. Even such great people as Abraham, Isaac, Jacob and Joseph did not follow him in all that they did. Abraham reckoned he needed to take a second wife to get a son when God had already promised him descendants from his first wife; he wasn't prepared to trust in the Lord God. Isaac allowed his sons to manipulate him to gain the inheritance; Jacob was a cheat and a deceiver; Joseph married a woman who did not follow the Lord. The family that should have been a blessing to all the world ended up down in Egypt, eventually becoming slaves of the Egyptians – of which more in a moment.

Then came Moses who was given the Torah. And the great family of Abraham had become a nation, the people of the book. But it still didn't work out. The people that were supposed to be the solution were part of the problem. At one time in their history it was said that 'all the people of Israel did what was right in their own eyes'[66].

The prophets saw what was happening and tried their best to get the people of God to follow him, as they should. One of the prophets said,

'This is what the LORD says: I will not revoke the punishment, because they have rejected the law of the Lord, and have not kept his statutes, but their lies have led them astray, those after which their fathers walked. So I will send a fire upon Judah, and it shall devour the strongholds of Jerusalem." Thus says the Lord: "For three transgressions of Israel, and for four, I will not revoke the punishment, because they sell the righteous for silver, and the needy for a pair of sandals – those who trample the head of the poor into the dust of the earth and turn aside the way of the afflicted; a man and his father go in to the same girl, so that my holy name is profaned.'[67]

But they refused to listen to what the prophets said. The prophets continually threatened and warned the people but it made no difference. Finally the prophets said that God was going to use the great empires of the Assyrians and the Babylonians from the north as his servants to punish Israel. One of them said, speaking for God, 'Therefore my people go into exile for lack of knowledge; their honoured men go hungry, and their multitude is parched with thirst. Man is humbled, and each one is brought low, and the eyes of the haughty are brought low. But the Lord of hosts is exalted in justice, and the Holy God will be proved holy by his righteous acts.'[68]

And using the imagery of a river he said, 'the Lord is bringing up against them the waters of the River, mighty and many, the king of Assyria and all his glory. And it will rise over all its channels and go over all its banks, and it will sweep on into Judah, it will overflow and pass on, reaching even to the neck, and its outspread wings will fill the breadth of your land, O Immanuel!'[69]

The descendants of Abraham, the family that should have brought blessing to the world, became slaves, exiles and refugees in Assyria and Babylon.

This was the second time the people of God were taken as slaves to conquering empires: first Egypt then Assyria and Babylon. Disaster after disaster. God had brought them back from Egypt in the redemption that is called the

Exodus. But they had not learned their lesson. They were conquered and taken into exile in Babylon because of their sinfulness. They came back from there in what is called the return from Exile and continued to sin. There seemed to be no way the people of the earth could be blessed as Abraham had been promised?

But yes, there was! A people, a nation, had failed. In the purposes of God one man would succeed where they had failed. Jesus was born, through his mother and adopted father, son of David, son of Abraham. By his works and his words he proved himself to be the one true Israelite, the only true member of the people of God. He was the pure, clean, perfect man, not seeking position and power, but caring for ordinary people, speaking to them in words and images they could understand, healing them, blessing them, loving them. Only he could bring about the fulfilment of the ancient promise to Abraham. All the problems, all the sins, all the curses of the world were placed on his shoulders that blessing might come to all." He paused and looked at Gaius and Anna to see how they reacted. There was silence.

Then Gaius started to express his thoughts, hesitantly and quietly as he began to understand God's great plan for the blessing of all peoples.

"That explains why and when Jesus died, right enough. But it still scarcely explains what his death accomplished, does it?" There was another pause and then he added, "What did his death achieve? I still don't see."

"Well" Jacob replied. "It is easiest to explain in terms of sacrifice. You know the way sacrifices have been important for the people of God since before the time of Abraham. Abraham carried out sacrifices and was even prepared to sacrifice his son when told to do so. He only did not do so because the Lord God stopped him. Later on Moses organized what was to be done and wrote down rules and regulations for what, and when, and how the sacrifices were to be made.[70]

The sacrifices were made both to please God and to turn aside sin. The animal sacrificed as a sin-offering carried the sin of the one who offered it. That was symbolized in the marvellous picture of the scape-goat on the annual Day of Atonement. Two goats were sacrificed in very different ways on that great day. One goat was sacrificed on the altar as the sacrifice for sin. Then the high priest laid his hands on the head of the second goat to symbolize the placing of all the sins of the people on the animal. It was taken out of the camp, far away into the desert, so far that it could never find its way back. The way those two animals were treated made it clear to all the people that there had to be a death to atone for sin and that when the death occurred the sin was taken a long way away never to be seen or considered again. It was forgiven. It was made abundantly clear to all the people that sin was dealt with.

Jesus gave some clear indications that his death was to be understood as a sacrifice for sin. He said that he came 'to give his life as a ransom for many'.[71] He told his disciples to remember that his blood had been 'poured out for many for the forgiveness of sins'. [72]

He taught his immediate disciples about his death and resurrection. Peter told the crowds a very few weeks after the death and resurrection of Jesus, '"Repent and be baptized every one of you in the name of Jesus Christ for the forgiveness of your sins.'[73] And 'turn again, that your sins may be blotted out.'[74] Jesus died for our sins and to make us acceptable to God.

This is the really exciting thing about Jesus. He died in our place. If we accept that and take it to our hearts, and live our lives in obedience to him we shall be able to approach the Lord God on the Day of Judgement with happy confidence that we shall be accepted. His death will be for us, each of us individually, if we believe in Jesus the Messiah and obey and follow him. We shall not be rejected and we will be allowed into his eternal kingdom."

"I think you want me to become a Christian," said Gaius with a smile. "Your enthusiasm is overwhelming!"

Jacob looked serious. "I don't want you to say you are a Christian because of my enthusiasm, young man. Indeed, I must apologize if it sounds that way. Remember that it is no easy thing to be known as a Christian. All too many of us have been killed and tortured because we have followed Jesus. Some of the followers of Jesus have been taken by the Roman authorities and challenged about their beliefs. They have said that Jesus is Lord and have not been prepared to say Caesar is Lord because they have only one Lord. They have been killed for doing that! Think long and hard before you take his name upon your lips."

"Can I ask a question," said Anna, rather hesitantly. "Why did sacrifices take away sin? For some time I have understood that the Bible says they do but I cannot see why. The animal sacrificed is a substitute for the person who offers it. But can it really pay for your sinfulness, anyone's sinfulness."

"Yes," said Jacob. "You are quite right. It is far too small a thing to pay for sin. But that is not what it did, and does. Our sin is forgiven because God makes us a free gift of forgiveness. That is the only way we could be forgiven. To say, as some people do, that we only have to do some good things to balance out the bad things we do is to totally misunderstand how pure and holy God is. We could never stand before him on the basis of the little things we have done. Forgiveness can never be bought by animal sacrifice, or any other way. The death of the sacrifice in the old days was a token of human repentance, of saying we are sorry for the way we have offended a holy God, and a token of God acting in forgiveness. The sacrifices were a continual reminder of their human sin and God's free forgiveness.

Things are different now. The sacrifice for our sins has been made – nearly 70 years ago now – when Jesus died on the cross. That happened once. It can never be repeated and doesn't need to be repeated. There are no more sacrifices. All that has to happen is that in our hearts and with our lips we have to express our allegiance to Jesus and then two things are ours: forgiveness of sin and the gift of the Holy Spirit.

Although I must add there is a mystery here. We have never been told why sacrifice takes away sin. The Bible nowhere makes that clear. Remember, Gaius, when we first met you said I had a reputation for saying that I don't know when I don't know. That is what I am doing now if you will forgive me!"

This last was said with a very kind and gracious smile at Gaius who smiled back and said, "Of course."

"But Jesus not only died for our sins he rose again from the dead. If we are identified with him in his death we will also be identified with him in his resurrection.[75] That means that we are accepted by God as righteous because he is accepted by God as the perfect righteous man. It also means that we have the power within us that he had to live a life which is well pleasing to God."

"What does 'righteous' mean?" asked Gaius.

"Yes, a difficult word! Basically it means doing right and being right. But it has come to mean being declared right and accepted by God as one of his people and therefore within his covenant, which, of course, implies doing right and being right. Only if we are righteous have we a hope of entry into his great Kingdom one day. And that is a great hope. 'Declared' and 'accepted' are the key words."

"So it means something that happens to us not something that we do," said Gaius in a rather puzzled tone of voice.

"Yes! It means being right in the sense of being good people. But we can only be good people when we have been declared right on the basis of what Christ has done."

"But we can only be righteous if we do right things," insisted Gaius.

"You don't really think you can do enough right things to be accepted by the totally holy, righteous Lord God, do you? You surely don't think you can ever hope to be that good, do you? Don't you realize that is a hopeless quest before you even start?"

Gaius had to laugh. "Alright. I suppose the answers have to be – no, no and yes. You are saying that the hope of so many people that they can be righteous enough to be accepted by God is all wrong, aren't you?"

"Yes, I am. Paul said, echoing the Psalmist 'there is no-one righteous, not even one.'[76] People have so much ability to delude themselves. No-one, but no-one, is ever going to be good enough to be accepted by God. We can only be accepted if God accepts us in spite of who and what we are. That is what he does as a result of Jesus dying on the cross. Jesus paid the price for our sins; he bought our righteousness at the price of his own blood. Why do people find that so hard to understand?"

Suddenly they were interrupted. There was a loud hammering on the front gate and shouts could be heard from outside. The three of them looked at each other.

"Another search party", said Jacob. "Open the gate, Anna, and then get out of sight."

Anna ran to the gate and lifted the bar.

6

The gate burst open and three Roman soldiers strode in. The senior man was a very tough looking character with many scars on his face and legs. The other two were less intimidating, much younger, almost boyish looking. But their sudden appearance was very alarming for the three in the courtyard.

At a signal from the leader the other two started moving round the edge of the yard opening doors and peering into rooms.

The senior man glanced at Jacob and looked with a slightly leering expression at the rapidly disappearing figure of Anna as she fled to the kitchen. He turned back to look hard at Gaius in whom he was obviously much more interested.

Jacob started to speak but was cut short by the leader who barked at Gaius, "Who are you?" in no friendly tone of voice.

"Gaius Severus, from Sidon," replied Gaius. He was trying hard not to betray the fear and anxiety he felt at this intrusion.

"Really!" in a mocking tone of voice. The close inspection continued. He then said rather grudgingly and as if disappointed, "though I suppose you do not fit the description we have been given: 'short, scar on left cheek, about 30 years old.'"

Jacob decided it was safe to say something now. "Who are you looking for," he asked. "We are residents here and I am sure there is no need to be concerned about our guest."

The leader of the soldiers looked hard at him, then glanced at a small piece of wood he had in his hand which, presumably, had something written on it. "Jacob Bar Joseph?" he said, more as a question than a statement.

"Yes, that's me," replied Jacob. "Sorry, I don't know you though I do know some of your comrades in the barracks." As he spoke he was trying to keep his voice pleasant and even tempered for he knew too well what trouble there could be for even the most innocent of people from a visit like this.

The other two soldiers reappeared followed by an obviously reluctant Anna.

"Nobody. Nothing," reported one of them.

The leader nodded slightly in reply. "You are some of these Christians, I believe," he said. "Not a good thing to be these days." It was noticeable that some of the bite had gone out of his voice.

"Yes," said Jacob, with a half-smile. "You know something of us then – but before you answer may I send Anna to get you some wine and biscuits?"

"That would be very welcome."

Jacob indicated that they were to sit at the table, which they did quite eagerly, and Anna disappeared rapidly into the kitchen. Jacob indicated to Gaius that he was to sit too and joined them himself. Anna reappeared very quickly with a large pitcher, 5 beakers and a plate of biscuits on a tray, placed them on the table in front of Jacob and moved back into the shadow where she could see but not be too obviously seen.

"Help yourselves," said Jacob with a smile. The leader immediately did so, then pushed the pitcher across to his men. There was silence as they drank and ate. Eventually the leader belched noisily and leant back.

"Drop of good stuff that," he remarked. "Who do you know at the barracks then?"

"Marcus and Patrobas, best," said Jacob being careful to only name those he knew were well known to be

Christians.

"Marcus is a good fellow even if he does have strange ideas," was admitted somewhat grudgingly. Turning to Gaius and speaking in a not now too unfriendly tone, "And what about you? Are you one of this lot too?"

"No, I am not a Christian," replied Gaius, but, after a short pause "I think I soon shall be one!" He didn't see Anna's slight start and then the big smile that spread across her face when he said this.

"You be careful, lad. Getting mixed up with that lot won't do your long term prospects any good at all!" said the leader of the soldier's, but not in an unfriendly way. "Anyway," turning to Jacob, "Do you know anything of this fellow we are looking for? He is called Jesus, same as your prophet."

"Is that Jesus BarJudas?" asked Jacob. The leader nodded. "Nothing that isn't common knowledge. He is a nasty man. He is said to have killed as many Jews as Romans. He has issued threats to some Christians we know in the next village. None of us would be sorry to see him caught and dealt with, much as we try not to condemn anybody. I would even go so far as to say we would tell you if we heard anything that would lead you to him. He is that bad."

The leader grunted in reply. "I'm glad to hear it. Come on you two we must be off. Thanks for the grub. It almost makes me think well of you lot."

The three men got up and disappeared out of the gate leaving it swinging loose behind them. Anna immediately shut it and locked it behind them, sat down at the table and challenged Gaius. "What did you mean by that? Are you going to join us? Have you decided that Jesus is Lord?"

"Hold on, girl," said Jacob with a smile, "not so fast. Though I would not mind hearing what you mean myself!"

Gaius hesitated and looked quite uncertain of what to say. "I don't know why I said that," he admitted. "I really hadn't thought it out beforehand. It just kind of slipped out as if somebody else put the words into my mouth." He looked quite embarrassed.

"Well, maybe somebody else did put the words into your mouth," said Jacob.

"Who do you mean?" The question burst out of both Gaius and Anna at the same time.

"I mean that is the sort of thing the Holy Spirit of Jesus does at some strange times like this," replied Jacob. "He is God at work in our lives even when we don't recognize him. It may well be that he put those words into your mouth. If he did, that means you are being called by God into his Kingdom."

"Hey, steady on," said Gaius. "I don't even know what it means to be a Christian, or how I could become a Christian. What I would need to do, and so on. All we have talked about so far is who Jesus was and what he did. We haven't talked at all about what it would mean to become a Christian. It would need to be something very important since it could lead to me losing my life from what I hear. That guy wasn't very encouraging after all. I have heard terrible stories about what has happened to some Christians."

The strain had obviously had an effect on Jacob but he managed to say, "I think we should have something to eat ourselves. Wait until the excitement and tension inside us from having them burst in like that has quietened down a bit and then we will start our serious talking again and try to answer those specific questions for you. Come on, Anna, clear this stuff away please and get us something to help us calm down after all that excitement."

Anna got up, smiling and looking very excited and happy. She cleared the table and quickly disappeared back into the kitchen area.

7

Very soon Anna had some food on the table and they sat eating, drinking and chatting quietly. They were all trying to calm their nerves after the interruption. Eventually Jacob thought it was time to start back into their discussion. He decided it was best to do this by tackling the questions Gaius had raised in his surprising outburst.

"You asked what it means to become a Christian," he said. There was a long pause.

"Yes!" said Gaius, slowly. "The way those people in Sidon were living was so good and then the things you have said seem to me to make very good sense. You are saying that who Jesus was and what happened to him are firm facts of history. I find that an argument it is very difficult to ignore.

What would I have to do to be a Christian? What are the rules and regulations of living as a Christian? What are the initiation ceremonies like? What would I have to give up to be a proper Christian?"

Jacob and Anna looked at each other. A half smile came on Jacob's face. Anna looked both excited and puzzled at the same time.

"Where to begin is a problem itself," said Jacob slowly. "Most of the questions you ask have no direct answer! Let me see." He paused, obviously thinking hard how best to explain the Christian life.

"I think we should take your question rather carefully. The 'how' you live as a Christian is much more important than the 'what' you do as a Christian but it is easier to take the 'what' first and then the 'how'.

Being a Christian is all about following Jesus. It is about being a member of his royal kingdom. Jesus set up the kingdom when he was here on earth and called people into it. He wanted people to think of themselves as subjects in the Kingdom of God and to owe allegiance to him as the Crown Prince in exactly the same way they would in any other kingdom. He, or she, as his subject must live in the right way within his Kingdom and be prepared to answer his call to battle."

He looked across at Gaius, who was looking puzzled, and stopped to see what he would say.

"Kingdom?" he said. "What kingdom? I don't see any kingdom around here except Herod's and that is really just part of the Empire of Rome. Rome rules. How can Jesus have a kingdom when Rome rules? I don't see any kingdom that is his. Indeed if I did it would be a contradiction of much of what you have said. How could he ever have a kingdom if it is to be a peaceful kingdom in which there is to be no fighting? Every kingdom I have ever heard of has been carved out of an existing kingdom by a warrior king with much fighting and many people killed. Every kingdom has an army to fight for it and an army of tax collectors to get the money the king needs to live in arrogant splendour. Kingdoms are not altogether a good thing!"

"All you have said is right," agreed Jacob, "that is how kingdoms operate in this world. We all know what a kingdom is. It is where a king tries to have total control over everything that happens. He rules. Everybody else is his subject. And it is very dangerous to do anything that challenges that rule. You and I are citizens of the Roman Empire. We are supposed to say 'Caesar is Lord' if we are asked to do so. Failure to do so by many Christians has led to persecution and death. We refuse to say 'Caesar is Lord' because Jesus is our only Lord, or King, or Prince over the Kingdom of God.

But the kingdom Jesus was talking about was, and is, a quite different sort of kingdom. It is a kingdom in people's hearts. It is an everlasting kingdom. It started as small as the smallest seed in just one city, Jerusalem, and it is growing and will grow until it covers all the world. One day people from every tribe and nation and people group will be in it. It is a quiet kingdom, which, like Jesus, does not make a big noise in the world. It grows like bread dough with yeast in it – you cannot see what is happening but you can see the dough growing and like to eat the result!

One day it will cease being hidden and be clearly seen by all people. That is the day when the King, Jesus, will return to this earth in splendour and everyone will have to acknowledge him as who he really is. He made the astounding claim that he is to be the judge of all the world when he said in answer to a question: 'the Father – by which he meant God – judges no one, but has entrusted all judgment to the Son – by which he meant himself'. Then he went on to say 'I tell you the truth, a time is coming and has now come when the dead will hear the voice of the Son of God and those who hear will live. And he has given him authority to judge because he is the Son of Man.[77]'"

"Now you have got me really confused," complained Gaius, "son of the Father, Son of God, son of Man – what a confusion of sons! What do they all mean?"

Jacob smiled. "Sorry!" he said. "I have to admit, that is a bit difficult. Jesus referred to God Almighty as his Father in a very special way related, of course, to the very special role he knew he had. He called himself the Son of God because he was the King Messiah and therefore in direct descent from the ancient kings of Israel who were called 'sons of God'. Remember we decided it was a status rather than anything else. He called himself the 'son of Man' because of a prophecy in the Bible which talks about a person called 'the son of man' who conquers all the evil powers of this world[78] – which is, of course, precisely what he did.

Chapter 7

It might have been better if I had just described what Jesus said rather than given you the actual words, but I do think his own words are very important."

Gaius cheered up. "OK," he said, "I get what you are saying – I think. Jesus claimed to be going to sit in judgment over everybody at the Day of Judgment. How on earth could he do that? What proof is there that can possibly be the case?"

"The proof is his resurrection," replied Jacob instantly, "The ancient prophecies have long said that one day there will be a day of resurrection when all the dead will be raised to be judged and receive the due reward for the way they have lived here on earth in this life. All the dead will be raised, that is everybody except one, who has already been raised ahead of everybody else. And, of course, you know who that one is!"

"Oh, yes, I see," said Gaius. "You mean he went on ahead of everyone else to get everything ready for the Day of Judgment."

"Well, yes. That is not the way it is usually put but it will do as a picture of what has happened and what is still to happen,"

Anna interrupted, "Haven't you two wandered off the point a bit," she asked with a grin. "I thought we were supposed to be talking about the things we need to do to be true followers of Jesus."

Jacob smiled at her, showing for a moment the love of a grandfather for a granddaughter. "Yes, in a sense, we are off the immediate point but what we are talking about is the hugely important background. All that we do as Christians we do because Jesus is our king and will be our judge in that day. We want to be able to look him in the face and not have to slink away ashamed of what we have done or, worse still, be condemned to a life in the fire or the shadows, banished for ever from the presence of all that is good and holy."

"So," he continued, "To get back to our main argument. First, in a very real sense we do not do anything to become accepted by God. What has happened to secure our acceptance has all been done for us by Jesus. His sacrifice was a full and sufficient satisfaction for all our sin and rebellion. All we have to do is to accept that is the case: that we can do nothing and he has done it all."

He stopped and looking at Gaius, waited for a reaction from him.

"You mean, " he said hesitantly and then with a distinct note of surprise in his voice, "we have to do nothing?"

"Yes, that is exactly right. But people do find it very hard to get their minds round that idea. Everybody thinks we must have to do something, but how could we possibly do anything worthwhile in the eyes of a truly great and holy God? You have to have a rather low view of God to think a human being can do anything of significance to him! Nothing we can do up to and including giving our lives is sufficient to secure our acceptance by a holy and righteous God. All we can do is put our hope and trust in Jesus. And it is because that is not really doing anything very much that I started off with my first point as the things we do not do. We cannot earn our way into the favour of God and into heaven."

Jacob stopped again waiting for a response to show that Gaius had got his point before continuing.

"Yes, I see that. It is a strange new thought to me but it does make sense. If they would only stop and think about it people, many of them friends of mine, are wasting their time when they try to impress the one true God with all their religious activity. He is far too great for that. All we can do is trust him."

Jacob smiled, please that his student had got his point so well. "That is the first and fundamental point. Only when we have accepted that there is nothing that we can do to secure our acceptance, then, and only then, there are things that we do. In fact there are no set rules and regulations about being a Christian in the sort of sense that you have asked. Jesus made it quite clear that the first and greatest rule is the double commandment to love. He said we are to love the Lord our God, the Creator God, the God of Abraham, Isaac and Jacob, and that we are to love our neighbours as ourselves. He took those two commands, one of them rather obscure, out of the books of Deuteronomy[79] and Leviticus[80] linked them together and gave them to us as the most important commandments."[81]

"What do you mean by 'love'?" asked Gaius. "I really haven't associated what I think of as love with things religious – even although I have heard about those two statements in the ancient books."

Jacob chuckled. "Good point, young man! And not an easy question to answer. I think of it this way. It is the sort of relationship you have in a family – a good family that is. You are in a family whether you like it or not. You cannot say 'you are no longer my brother' to your brother. You are stuck with him as your brother forever. The bond between the two of you cannot be broken any more than the bond between two sisters or a brother and a sister can be. You are responsible for each other; you support each other; you help each other; you have to live together even if you are not the sort of people who would have chosen to live together; you especially support each other when you are ill, or weak or very young, or old; you maintain the family honour; you avoid bringing shame on the family. In all those things in a very practical way you live in relationship to each other. Of course, I am talking about a rather ideal family. Because of the essential sinfulness of human nature it often isn't quite like that in practice. But you can only define love in relation to someone else. It does not exist by itself.

So I have to use an illustration. That, I think, is what talking about love in a Christian way means. When Jesus talked about loving other people he meant that you treat other people in exactly the same way as you treat those who are closest to you, those who are members of your own good family. You treat them as brothers and sisters."

"Wow!" said Gaius. "That is a great description. I will have to think that one over in detail, but I get your meaning enough for now."

He continued, "Are you saying that that is the only rule for Christians? I can see that it would cover a lot of behaviour, but life is easier if you know what you may, or may not, do. What did Jesus say about the Law of Moses that we have lived by for so long?"

"You are a very astute young man," acknowledged Jacob. "You keep on going right to the heart of things with your questions.

This one is not easy to answer either. In a way you could say that Jesus had three different laws in mind in the things he said. First there was the law God gave to Moses on Mount Sinai. Jesus honoured that but he pointed out what the real meaning of the law was. He explained how the commands of the law relate to what our deepest motives are as I explained when we were talking about sin. He wasn't satisfied with us just obeying the details of what it says we should do and not do. Then there was the law, as we know it in the Judaism of today. All sorts of things have been added to Moses' law to try and make sure that it is kept in every little particular act. It has become the sort of law that tries to regulate everything that everybody does. Such a law sounds very good but it never works in practice. There are always people in every society whose hearts are not right so they manipulate the law to their own advantage. They make life hard for other people who do not keep the law in exactly the way that they think is right. They like to keep the ceremonial parts of the law but ignore the parts that are about being good to other people. Unless the heart is right the motives are wrong and such laws do not bring people closer to God. Sometimes Jesus was really rather rude about some of the things that people teach about keeping the law.

He preached about the law of the Kingdom. He told us how to live the life of a Kingdom person owing allegiance to the Lord God.

But, wait a minute. I've been talking too much! It is time you said something! Tell me a law which started off as a good thing but has been turned into a burden that people find hard to bear."

There was a pause as the two young people thought about it. Gaius and Anna looked at each other to see who would speak first.

Eventually Gaius said, "I get very fed up with the Sabbath law. It makes no sense to me that we are not supposed to walk more than 2 kilometres on the Sabbath even if we are going to the synagogue or taking something important to somebody who is ill. Why shouldn't we?"

"Very good," said Jacob with a smile. "You have chosen one of the laws that Jesus himself criticized most, and for exactly the same reason. He healed a man on the Sabbath and when he was criticized for doing so asked: "Which is lawful on the Sabbath: to do good or to do harm, to save life or to kill?"[82] And he got into awful trouble with the religious leaders for that. He also said, "The Sabbath was made for man, not man for the Sabbath.[83] Jesus clearly put doing good things for other people above keeping the letter of the law. In other words he put love for other people higher than keeping the details of the law. He put the intent of the heart above the outward actions."

He paused. "Now, what about you, Anna? Can you think of something else?"

She thought for a moment. "I had the same idea as Gaius first. But, what about the food laws? All the Gentiles eat pig meat and it does them no harm! Why can't we? I was at the house of a friend who is not a Jew and they gave me some meat to eat. It tasted strange and they only told me afterwards that it was pig meat. I think they did it for a tease to see what I would say. It was rather nice actually. I enjoyed it and nothing bad happened to me!"

"That is a very interesting one," said Jacob. "I don't know why we were given that law in the first place but the way it is used now is to make a clear distinction between Jews and everybody else. I certainly don't think that was its original purpose. Now people like to think that they are good people of God just because they don't eat one particular sort of meat. That has nothing to do with love or with pure motives in the heart. It has become a way in which people build a sort of wall around Israel to keep everybody else out. One of the things Jesus did was to take every opportunity to break down that wall. He refused to see any difference before God between an Israelite and anybody from any other nation. The result of what Jesus did and said is that such laws no longer apply in the kingdom of God. Anybody and everybody can be a member of the kingdom of God."

"Do you mean I can do things like eat pork meat?" said Gaius, looking very puzzled and perplexed. "You mean I can do what I like if I become a Christian,"

Jacob smiled. "Yes and no," he replied. "This is a very good example of how the law of love works in practice. Jesus' teaching meant 'yes, you can eat pork' because it does not matter what goes into your mouth – at least as far as religious behaviour is concerned. It is what comes out of your mouth, the things you say, and the things you do, that determine what sort of person you are and therefore whether you are a good person or not in God's eyes.[84] But the answer can also be 'no' because we have to take our fellow believers, and those who are not yet believers, into consideration. One of the early apostles said 'The one who eats everything must not look down on one who does not, and the one who does not eat everything must not condemn the one who does, for God has accepted that person'[85]. That is a practical example of what Jesus meant when he said we must love our neighbours as ourselves. Don't upset other people unnecessarily. Always be kind to them. Always help them along life's way for that is difficult enough for all of us without being tripped up by other people."

He paused for breath. Gaius said nothing so he continued, "Of course Jesus was no sooner gone from this earth than those who wanted to follow him started to think up some rules to make it easier to think you are living as a proper Christian. It is always easier to have set rituals – special times and forms for prayers, things to eat and things not to eat, days to feast and days to fast. But the whole point of what Jesus taught us was that these are not the things that please God. He wants us for himself, the whole of us, not the things we do and say.

Remember that we talked about God and how he is not the remote figure that so many people think he is. And we did that when we were thinking about how Jesus said he was God in a roundabout sort of way.

Well, this was one of the most important things Jesus said. He argued as no one else has ever argued that God wants us to love him, to be faithful, to trust Him, and to be loyal to Him, and that we do these things by being good to other people. Our worship of him is to be shown in our love for other people. Which is far more difficult than just being religious. But your friends in Sidon seem to have been good at it."

Gaius still looked puzzled. "You mean," he said, slowly "that following Jesus is mainly a matter of living well with other people. Have I got that right?"

"Yes!" said Jacob. "Provided we do that for the right motives and because we are the right sort of people. Some people make sure they are good to other people because they want something for themselves. They have selfish reasons for what they do. They help other people in the hope that they can get some favour out of them later or sometimes they even do it because it makes them feel good to themselves.

Anna could keep silent no longer. "But, Grandpa, in that case why do we do so many things that other people don't do? We meet as often as we can, we sing songs to God and to Jesus in our worship, we listen to what you and the other teachers in the meeting have to say. Do you mean that really doesn't matter? I find that very puzzling when we spend so much time doing those things!"

"Oh," said Jacob, taken a bit by surprise and hesitating as he thought about what he had just said and how it related to what Anna was asking. "Well yes. I have been talking about the really basic things of what we are. You are talking about the ways in which we do things to help us with those basics. Yes – those things do matter, they matter a lot. But we can't be Christians by just doing those things. We have to live the life that Jesus set before us as the Way.

What we do in worship of God and of Jesus is very important because it reminds us who we are, it gives us the encouragement of being with other people who are on the same Way as we are and it informs us what we should be doing. More important still it reminds us continuously of where we are going."

Gaius spoke up, "Where we are going? What do you mean by that? And while I'm asking questions: what is the Holy Spirit?"

"Oh, dear," said Jacob. "It seems that I only answer one question to get two more in reply! But that is not meant to put you off. I'm very happy to answer as many of your questions as I can!

But just one more thing before we stop thinking about how we should live and what we should do. Don't get to thinking that because we focus on motives we can do all sorts of things. Paul used to give some quite long lists in his letters of things we should not do and things we should do. Some of them might surprise you. He told us obvious things not to do like sexual immorality or idolatry and then added in some much less obviously wicked things like gossiping and arguing![86] Things we should do include peace, patience and gentleness.[87]

We ought to go on to think about the Holy Spirit, but it is time for us to stop so Anna can get the evening meal. Her brothers and their wives will be coming round to join us. Can you not stay with us any longer tomorrow?"

"I would love to do so, but I really can't. My father will be expecting me back in about a week from when I left and I have another day's walking to do to get to Caesarea, I will need two days for my business, then two or three days back to Sidon. I will be able to hire a mule to ride on the way back, which will make it quicker. I know ..." brightening up, "I could stop overnight on the way back, if that is all right?"

"Of course. We would love to see you again. This is not a good point to stop our discussions. You actually said something suggesting you felt you might become a Christian and we need to follow that up. Think hard about what we have talked about while you are away.

Does your father know that you were going to stop here?"

"Sort of. He knows I was intending to stop to see you but not that I was going to get so much good hospitality from you and prolong my stay!"

"You are very welcome," added Anna.

"Is he happy about you exploring Christianity," asked Jacob, "or antagonistic?"

"Oh, he is quite happy. We have often talked together about how well the Christians in our city live. He will be very interested in what I will have to tell him about what you have told me."

"Good!" said Jacob, with a big smile. "Here is the rest of the family."

8

Into the courtyard came the two brothers with their wives and children. Gaius was introduced to Sarah, the wife of Matthew, and Rebekah, the wife of James. The four youngest children with them, all under the age of five, ran over to their great grandfather who had to hug them all at the same time. The eldest followed more slowly, obviously emphasizing he was a bit more grown up. Jacob was hauled away to play some game or other with them. The wives disappeared into the kitchen area with Anna. It became apparent that Anna who had been talking with Gaius and her grandfather most of the day was relying on them bringing food with them, which they had done.

Gaius sat down with the brothers who quizzed him about why he was there and what he was doing. He explained how he had stopped in the middle of his journey. That interested them as they were in the transport business and did much travelling. Gaius discovered that he had not come the quickest and easiest way even if it was the shortest. Then, when he explained how he hoped to stop on the way back but was short of time to do so, they soon worked out how it could be done in the time available. They told him they were going part of the way to Caesarea the next morning so they invited him to walk with them for the first part of his journey; an invitation that he gladly accepted. They told him where to hire a mule in Caesarea from a friend of theirs that could be left with them when he came back and promised him one of theirs for the onward journey. They told him they often went down to Sidon so he might even be able to travel with them that day. A short delay waiting for them would not matter, as he would have had to find a caravan to travel with the rest of his way home anyway for safety.

Gaius explained his business to the brothers. If he was successful there would be regular consignments going from Caesarea to Sidon so they were soon talking business: prices and possibilities. They took him round to the back of the house to see their stabling and the animals they had in them. He quickly realized that he was getting the perfect excuse to his father for his time spent stopped when he was supposed to be travelling! He promised them business if he got the trade he was hoping for.

The three of them returned round to the main courtyard and the dining room to find the meal was on the table. The children were called in. They appeared with a rather tired looking great grandfather. The usual chaos of getting young children sitting down and ready to eat ensued. But soon they were all seated, grace, the prayer before eating, had been said, and the meal commenced. They ate and talked. Gaius realized that the family were all Christians. Their attitudes to each other revealed a great deal of love and harmony even although they spent little time talking about specifically Christian things. Gaius revelled in it. He had seldom, if ever, been with such a happy and united family. The youngsters were given temporary beds before long and the adults talked on. Gaius did not notice the way in which the others were watching to see how he and Anna were relating to each other.

Eventually everyone had stopped eating. The three women cleared up the meal and disappeared together to wash up. When they were finished it was time for the two couples to retrieve their children and carried them away to their own homes. Jacob retired to bed. Gaius and Anna, rather reluctantly, went away to their beds too.

Gaius was up much earlier the next morning than he had been the previous day. By the time he had had his breakfast the brother's mule train was ready so he said his goodbyes to Anna and Jacob and left with them. As he went he

Chapter 8

realized how well he had fitted in with the family there and how happy he had been with all that had happened.

For the first part of the journey Gaius was talking to one or both brothers almost all the way so he did not have any real opportunity to reflect on his two days with Jacob and Anna. Once he had said goodbye to them and continued his journey with another caravan they had introduced him to, he enjoyed the time for reflection that a long walk affords. His thoughts went round and round between the Christian things they had discussed and thoughts of Anna. He surprised himself at first by how much he kept thinking about her. He wanted to think about the things of God and about faith but she kept popping up in his mind.

That was the pattern, not only of the journey time, but also of the next two days in Caesarea. Gaius concluded that Anna was different and most of the difference was because of her Christian faith. She was more confident of herself as a person than most young women he had met; she was more ready to express her thoughts; she was strong with the sort of strength of character he greatly admired. He was slowly working towards only one possible conclusion.

His business negotiations were successful. He had come in the hope of being able to secure from the upper Jordan valley a supply of good quality papyrus reed for making writing paper. His father had been buying it from Egypt but reckoned they ought to be able to find it much cheaper more locally if they could find a supplier who had the right conditions to grow it in. They had heard that there was such a situation near Caesarea. The only question was whether the quality was good enough and that was difficult to judge. So he was taking as much as a mule could carry behind its rider back to their small workshop in Sidon so that they could make papyrus paper with it and get a conclusive test of its quality and suitability. He agreed with the man who was growing it in his reed beds that if all went well they would both be able to expand their operations very considerably to their mutual benefit.

So after his day's walk down to Caesarea and two days in the town he set off the next day on a hired mule back to the village.

The mule was not pleased at how fast it had to walk.

Gaius discovered Jacob and Anna at their evening meal when he finally got back to their house. They seemed to him to be as delighted to see him, as he was to see them. Before he could sit down his mule had to be put in the stables and fed. When he went round the back with it he was delighted to find Matthew there. He reported his success as they unloaded his reed bundles. Matthew offered to see to his mule so that he could go and eat and he was very glad to do that. He sat down at the table and realized that Anna had cooked enough stew in the pot to allow for his presence. She had expected him back. Stew and wine and figs and dates were very welcome as he had had nothing much to eat on the journey.

Jacob and Anna had seen, and were puzzled by, the large bundles of reed on the mule as he came into the house so he had a considerable amount of explaining to do. By the time he had finished it was well after sunset so they did not renew their more formal discussions. Gaius explained that he ought to leave the following midday so they decided they would have another session the following morning. Then they all went to their beds.

9

They were up early the next morning. As soon as breakfast was finished and cleared away the three of them sat down together to continue their discussions.

"I will not ask you yet what your thoughts have been," said Jacob. "Let's finish our discussion about the main teachings of the Christian faith first. Where had we got to?" he asked, though Gaius had a shrewd suspicion that he knew very well!

"You mentioned the Holy Spirit as we stopped," he said anyway. "What is the Holy Spirit?"

"What is the Holy Spirit," repeated Jacob thoughtfully. "We had plenty of difficult questions before. But this is just as hard as any of those!" he said with a grin so he was clearly not disturbed by it.

"Actually, we refer to the Holy Spirit as 'he' but that is not worth going into just now.

The point is this: we have been talking about all these fine things one should do to live properly in the kingdom and to be like Messiah Jesus, but it is impossible for ordinary human beings like you and me to do them all. Nobody is that good, except Him. We need help. And that help comes from God himself. We call the God who helps 'the Holy Spirit'."

"Is this a third God, then," asked Gaius a little mischievously. "Or the third pile of lentils?"

Jacob caught the fact this was a bit of a tease and was not put out by it.

"As I am sure you have already seen, young man, NO! And yes for the lentils. If Jesus was God, the one and only God, the embodiment of God on earth, but not God the Father, fully God, yet part of God, then there is a place for the Holy Spirit. He is how God makes himself known to us while still being transcendent, far above us and beyond our comprehension.

Just before Jesus was killed he talked to his disciples about another 'Helper'[88] who would come after him. He was quite specific about that. We understand that the person he talked about is of the same sort as he was. That means that since Jesus was God, and is God, so is this person. We call him the Holy Spirit. Indeed we often call God 'the Father, the Son and the Holy Spirit': one God with a three fold name and three ways of relating to us. Thus what we often say in blessing as we part from each other is 'May the grace of the Lord Jesus Christ, and the love of God, and the fellowship of the Holy Spirit be with you'.

Another way of thinking about him is as 'the Spirit of Jesus'.

Everybody's problem when they start to follow the way of Jesus is that we can't do it; it is too difficult. The solution is that we get the Spirit inside us to teach us and guide us. That makes us a new sort of person altogether. Jesus talked about that. He talked about being born again, by which he meant restarting life as a different sort of person as if you were starting again from the cradle.[89] He talked about his disciples being as intimately connected to him as a branch of a tree is to the trunk.[90] He talked about them being thirsty and drinking from him and then being so full of the Spirit that it was like having a spring of life-giving water within them.[91] The Holy Spirit of Jesus is unseen, often not noticed; He is God, quietly working in our lives."

Jacob hesitated, obviously thinking deeply, and confessed, "I am finding all this difficult to make clear."

He looked at Gaius, as if he was trying to see right into him. So much so that Gaius started to feel quite uncomfortable and Anna noticed both her grandfather's intensity and Gaius' discomfort. Eventually she could stand the silence no longer. "What's up Grandpa?" she asked, looking and sounding very puzzled.

Jacob half smiled and made up his mind. "Gaius," he said, "let me guess. Why did you come here? It was a strange thing to travel so far, just on the off chance of learning more about Christians and their Way. Why didn't you just ask around in Sidon? Did something else happen that you have not told us about that sent you on this difficult and dangerous quest?"

Gaius looked very surprised at these questions and then flushed and looked embarrassed. "Well," he said, and paused, looked at them both, then continued very hesitantly unlike his usual confident self, "It was like this – there was more to it. I had a dream. In fact, I had it, the same dream, more than once. It kept coming back to me. I couldn't get away from it. It consumed me. It was more like a vision than a dream. It made me come here."

Anna stared at him and burst out impatiently, "Go on! What was the dream?"

Gaius turned towards her and spoke to her, perhaps because he found it easier to tell her than Jacob what had happened. "I saw a man. I kept on seeing this man. He was a small man, a hill man from the way he looked and walked. He had rough and dirty clothes as if he was doing a lot of walking on dusty roads. Although he was small and apparently inconspicuous there was something special about him. A group of men and women was following him in my dream. Sometimes I saw him sitting down and teaching them as they sat in a circle around him. He was very obviously the most important person there.

Then I had another dream. He came right up to me and looked hard at me." Gaius paused, struggling with what he had to say next. "I asked him: 'Who are you?' And he replied: 'I am Jesus. Go. Find out about me. Ask who I am.' The dream, or vision, faded and I woke up. I felt very tense and excited and convinced that I was on the edge of something very important and thrilling.

That is when I started asking who would tell me about Jesus. That is why I came to see you." He stopped abruptly and looked at them both. Anna was obviously very excited by what she heard and glanced across at her grandfather.

Jacob smiled a slow happy smile. "I guessed right," he said, "or perhaps the Lord led me to ask. That was the work of the Holy Spirit in your life. That was God working in your life even before you were one of His people.

Sometimes God speaks to us like that. Sometimes indirectly, perhaps by what people like us, Anna and I, say that touches someone's heart and life in a deep and special way for which there is no natural explanation. That is the work of the Holy Spirit.

"You are saying, then," said Gaius, "that God the Holy Spirit actually spoke to me personally." There was a hint of doubt in his voice as he struggled to think that was possible.

"Yes, he is the quiet part of God. He is like the woman who works in the kitchen, seldom, or never seen in the front of the house by the visitors but the person without whom the whole house and home would not work!"

"Not like Anna, then," Gaius could not resist replying, "she makes far too much noise in the front of the house!"

Jacob laughed heartily at this. Anna tried to look quiet and demure, but, failing completely, broke into laughter as well. They all enjoyed the release of tension from the deep things they had been talking about.

"Oh, I agree," said Jacob, "but I do like her this way."

"So do I," agreed Gaius, without thinking what he was saying. He stopped and nearly apologized, then decided not to. He glanced sideways at Anna who had blushed and looked down. There was a moment's awkwardness between them. Jacob realized what had happened and spoke to break the silence.

"Seriously, though, I hope you get my point. Jesus himself told us that the Holy Spirit would come in his place. He told his disciples it was for their own good that he was going away. After all, the unseen Holy Spirit could do far more than one man could however powerful and tirelessly hard working that man might be. He does more than Jesus could do as he walked this earth because Jesus was limited to one place at a time. He does these things through us, which is why we spend so much time helping other people in their poverty and their illnesses.

He does what we could not do ourselves. Some people are good at talking to a big crowd. They use rhetoric and argue persuasively. But if they are talking about God and Christ their words will have no effect on their hearers unless the Holy Spirit is working through them and in their hearers. People hear many explanations about Jesus and it has no effect on them. The words are as much use as the noise a boy makes scaring crows. Then suddenly, one day, the Holy Spirit speaks to them and it all makes sense.

"Yes," interrupted Anna, "I have often heard people explaining how that is the sort of thing that happened to them. They tell of a special moment when it all began to make sense. I never knew why that happened before. I am learning such a lot by listening to you two talking."

This was said with a beautiful smile that had quite an effect on Gaius. "Does the Holy Spirit do anything else?" asked Gaius.

"Yes," replied Jacob, "he fills in the gaps in our knowledge. Here in the village we only have copies of two of the Gospels and of the letters Paul wrote to two of the very early churches– one of each is hidden in our roof, right now – so there are gaps in our knowledge of what Jesus taught and Paul taught, of how we should behave and understand the things that happen."

What's a Gospel?", asked Gaius.

"Oh, sorry, I should have explained. It is what we call the accounts that four men wrote of the life and death of Jesus, and of course, his resurrection.

If we don't know what we should do over some problem there are three people amongst us who are sometimes able to say something to fill in those gaps. When they do that we call it prophecy and understand that the knowledge comes to them straight from God by the work of the Holy Spirit."

"Does that include knowing what is going to happen?" asked Gaius.

"Sometimes. Not necessarily, and never completely. We are always very careful how we accept what is said about the future. And sometimes we reject it."

"Does the Holy Spirit do anything else?"

"Sometimes someone is healed of an illness or a disability. Two of us in our fellowship have been given something of a healing gift. Again we have to be very careful. There are plenty of charlatans around, both inside and outside the churches. But there are genuine healings given to us and we treasure the occasions when they are clearly seen to be a special work of the Holy Spirit in which things happen in much the same way that they did for Jesus. Only he could always heal people. We can only do so sometimes. Not that we actually do the healing ourselves; it is the Lord who uses us as a channel of blessing through healing."

"Errr, grandpa," said Anna, "I hate to stop you but isn't it about time for me to get the meal before Gaius goes.

"Oh, yes it is. But before we stop I want to ask Gaius what his thoughts are about becoming a Christian." He turned to Gaius. "Do you want Anna to hear what you want to say, or not? I think she would quite understand if you wanted your thoughts to be confidential."

Gaius smiled. "I will be quite happy for her to hear what I say. Not that I am going to say very much.

Chapter 9

I find all that we have talked about very compelling. But two things make me hesitate: that the possible consequences of becoming a Christian are quite enormous is the first and least important of them. But also from what I have said in passing at one time and another you will have guessed that I am very close to my father. I don't expect for one moment that he would stop me following the Way of Jesus but I would like to tell him what I intend to do before I do it. So my second reason for hesitating to say very much now is that: I want to tell him first." He spoke with an appeal in his voice.

He went on, "But I have started praying to the Lord Jesus and am very comfortable with doing that. Expect me to reappear very soon saying I am going to follow Jesus all the rest of my days!"

"Young man," replied Jacob, noticing as he spoke that a big smile had spread across Anna's face as Gaius talked, "What you say does you great credit. I am not going to try and get you to say any more than that before you go. The Lord will speak to you far better than I can. Let us pray together before we do anything else:

Our great Creator and Saviour God, our Father in heaven, we honour and praise you. Lord Jesus we honour and praise you. We rejoice in the things concerning yourself that we have been talking and thinking about this past week. Now as the time comes for us to part we, Anna and I, pray for this young man Gaius. It is our heart's desire that you will speak to him from your grace and goodness; that he will respond with true faith and faithfulness; that he may become a true and worthy servant of yours; that he may have good and happy conversations with his father and family when he gets home; that your care and protection may be upon him as he travels. That yours may be all the glory, Amen."

Jacob gave Gaius a great big hug. Anna wanted to do so

too but decided it would be a bit too forward so she hurried away to the kitchen before she did anything wrong. Gaius just about had tears in his eyes.

It was a somewhat subdued threesome who sat down to eat their lunch together. All too quickly it was time for Gaius to go. He went through and loaded his mule, came back into the courtyard, said his farewells and moved towards the gateway. As he did so he managed to grasp Anna's elbow without being seen, as a kind of token hug. He was careful not to look back until he was nearly out of sight and no one could see how moved he was.

10

Only ten days later just as Jacob, Anna and Anna's mother Martha were sitting down to an early evening light meal there was a thunderous but joyful knocking on the door. Anna ran to open it hoping it was Gaius. It was, on a mule this time. They grinned delightedly at each other without saying anything. Gaius greeted Jacob and was introduced to Martha. Martha and Gaius examined each other. Martha had heard quite a lot about Gaius in the days since she had returned and Gaius was curious to meet her. He certainly liked what he saw. There was a clear resemblance between Martha and Anna. Martha was a little shorter and rounder with a quiet and peaceful sort of character though evidently not shy.

After these greetings were over Jacob turned to Gaius. "We, the Christians in the village, are meeting tonight, here, in our house. Would you like to meet with them? We have to be careful who we allow into our meetings, trying to make sure they are genuine seekers and not spies for the Romans or the religious authorities who try to stop us and get information about who is involved. But I am happy that you are who you say you are and are really here for the best of reasons. Your story is too unusual to be made up! And my instinct, or is it the Holy Spirit, tells me you are thoroughly genuine."

Gaius raised his hands in a self-deprecating gesture. "I would be delighted to. Can I help with the getting ready? What do you have to do?"

"No," said Anna. "Have something to eat first. As you can see we are only having a light meal for there will be a fellowship meal when everybody is here. Then you can help. Come on, eat up."

"I think I had better see where my mule has gone to first," he suggested with a grin. "They are chancy beasts to let wander off as that one has done." So he went and stabled and fed it at the back of the house.

As soon as he could he was back round at the table. He probably ate too much, too swiftly, trying to answer questions as to what had happened in the intervening days at the same time. He reported that the papyrus reeds had proved thoroughly satisfactory so they were going to be buying a lot more from Caesarea. Anna was delighted to hear that. He showed them two pieces of finished papyrus and gave them one. The other was to show to the supplier of the reeds.

As soon as he was finished he got his instructions from Anna. "We don't have much to do. We tidy up this courtyard. Set up two tables over here and two over there. Make sure there are beakers so that everybody gets a drink of watered wine when they arrive. I already have some food for later on ready round the back and more will be brought by some of the people coming. Some of it can come out on to those two tables immediately; some of it I will keep warm in the oven. We set up the vessels for our ceremonial feast over on that table and fetch one of the scrolls to put on the next table to it. Which scroll is it to be tonight, Grandpa?"

"Put out the scroll of the Gospel according to John, please, Anna."

"Oooh, good," she responded. She added for the benefit of Gaius, "That is the newest one we have. It only came in three weeks ago and it is so different and so exciting. We had it copied in Antioch. It was terribly expensive. It was a good job we had such a good harvest last year and everybody had some spare money that we could put towards getting it copied. One of the men from here went and did a lot of the copying which kept the cost down a bit."

She said all this as she was going to the kitchen so Gaius

did not have a chance to ask her some of the questions that sprang to his mind.

"Here," she called from one of the side rooms. "There are tables in here. These two go over there; those two over the other side."

Gaius carried the first one out. "Here?" he asked Jacob.

"A bit further back - that will do."

"And this one?"

"The other side and in line, close up to that one."

The bustle continued with the laying down of carpets, obviously for people to sit on. Gaius doing the carrying, Martha, Anna and Jacob directing. He knew the three of them would have had more difficulty moving things around had he not been there to help and was glad to be useful. It was a strange experience for him, used as he was to having slaves to do things like this, but he found it curiously satisfying to be involved.

He was very interested when Anna took him through to the back of the house, up some steps to the roof, went into the room there and opened a box. She took a scroll from it and gave it to him in a tube carefully wrapped in a soft leather covering. He took it down, put it on the table indicated, and removed it from the wrapping and the tube, as instructed. He looked longingly at the scroll.

He got his opportunity when Jacob said he wanted to go through to pray and get his thoughts together for what he wanted to say at the meeting.

"Please," he asked, "may I open the scroll and read from it, or do you only allow the priests to read it?"

"Bless you," replied Jacob. "Remember we have no priests, and, of course, you may read it. We have no rules that restrict people's access to the truth. Come. I will open it and suggest what you might like to read."

He took the scroll and carefully unrolled it. He took a long time searching through it for the bit he wanted.[92]

"Are, here it is! This is a very interesting story. Read from here." Pointing at the middle of a column and placing two short sticks on the scroll to keep it unrolled.

Gaius started to read, keeping his voice down, as the other three went through to other rooms to continue their preparations for the meeting.

"Now a certain man was ill, Lazarus of Bethany, the village of Mary and her sister Martha. It was Mary who anointed the Lord with ointment and wiped his feet with her hair, whose brother Lazarus was ill. So the sisters sent to him, saying, 'Lord, he whom you love is ill.'"[93] He read on, rapidly becoming engrossed in the story.

Gaius was not able to read very far before it became too dark to see the scroll properly. He was just about to stop when Anna came out with a large oil lamp, so big that it had three separate wicks burning. She put it down on the table by the scroll so he could see to read.

"I wish I could stop and listen to your reading," she said. "I have only heard that story once when we read quickly through the whole scroll, so I have not had time to think about it and try to work out what it all means. But I must get things ready." She started to go.

Gaius quickly called after her, "Can I help?"

She smiled, said "Not really", and disappeared again through to the back of the house. Gaius returned to his reading, grateful for the light.

Anna had no sooner finished her preparations and come back through when there was a gentle knock on the gate and the first visitors arrived. Gaius realized that the sun had gone down and it was now completely dark. He wondered whether the meeting was so late for security reasons. He knew that the Christians in the city of Sidon had to be very careful not to attract any unwanted attention to themselves but he was surprised to realize that they had to be equally careful in a village like this.

Chapter 10

Jacob came through as soon as he realized people were arriving and greeted them individually. Gaius noticed that he appeared to direct the visitors' attention to him and to say something he could not hear but he was not beckoned over so he settled down to his reading again. But he was too often distracted to make much sense of what he was reading so he gave up and settled down in a dark corner of the courtyard to watch the arrivals. His suspicions about their secretiveness were confirmed when he realized that, although some people were coming in through the front gate, others were arriving by some back entrance he had not seen.

His attention was particularly caught by a group of four people arriving that way. A man came in escorting three women all of whom had head-coverings pulled right over their faces as though they did not want to be seen. When they pulled their coverings back he could not help staring at them. They were young, about the same age, and all strikingly good looking. But there the resemblances ended. One of them was obviously a woman of some wealth, who had an expensive looking gold necklace glistening round her neck, hidden under her outer cloak. She looked as though she might be the wife or daughter of a Roman official or army officer. Her hair was dark and her skin colour showed that she came from somewhere south of where they were. One of the other woman was strikingly fair haired and fair skinned. Gaius realized with a start that this meant she must be a slave, probably from northern Europe, as indeed her clothing would also suggest. The third was as black a person as Gaius had ever seen, clearly from somewhere in Africa, and also presumably a slave. Yet the three of them immediately started chatting away much more like friends than mistress and slaves. Gaius made a mental note to ask Anna who they were.

He need not have bothered because, after greeting the

women and the man, Jacob beckoned him across to meet them

"This is Narcissus, the wife of Epenetus, the Roman assistant governor for this area," he told Gaius. "This is Tigist," indicating the dark girl, "and this is Freya. They are of the household of Narcissus, together with Aelfred, Freya's father."

Looking across at the strongly built man who had accompanied the women Gaius saw that he was also fair-haired and fair-skinned and a slave.

"Narcissus is a great help to us here, as she is able to give us some protection from any anti-Christian actions. She is a Christian herself, of course. Freya is a great help to, in a different way. She is a very able and intelligent girl – Freya blushed at this – who leads our worship and spends a lot of time visiting people and helping them. You will hear from her later in the evening. Tigist is a great musician who also takes an active part in our worship and work." He went on to explain to the women who Gaius was and how he came to be there that evening.

Gaius also saw that Matthew and James had arrived though he did not get a chance to speak to them.

Time passed. There was a quiet hum of conversation as people greeted each other and stood or sat in small groups talking. Two fellows about his own age came over and talked to Gaius but the conversation stayed on unimportant topics as they asked him about where he came from and what Sidon was like as a city. Eventually it was clear nobody had come in for some time so it looked like time to start.

Jacob said something Gaius did not hear to Freya and she darted into a side room, greeting Anna with great affection on the way, and reappeared carrying a large flute and a harp. She gave the harp to Tigist and they sat down cross-legged near to the central tables and started to play a quiet, haunting melody. The combination of the two instruments was very pleasing. Then he realized that a young man sitting in a corner in the dark was following them gently on a hand drum. They were evidently a well-practiced trio of musicians.

This was recognized as the signal that the meeting should start. Everyone began to sit down on the carpets. Gaius hesitated about where to put himself. He noticed immediately that there was a tendency for the women to sit one side and the men the other but it did not seem to be a strict arrangement. Indeed he saw that Anna was beckoning him over to sit by her so that she was on the edge of the women's area and he would be on the edge of the men's.

"I will explain what is happening," she whispered.

The three musicians finished the quiet music and started to play more loudly. One of the younger men started to sing in a sort of chant.

"Great indeed, we confess, is the mystery of godliness:

He appeared in the flesh, was vindicated by the Spirit,

Was seen by angels, preached among the nations,

Was believed on in the world, was taken up in glory."[94]

He sang it one line at a time; stopped; and everybody sang, repeating the line after him. Once he realized what was happening Gaius was happy to join in. The singing continued through two more verses before stopping.

The young man who had been singing asked Freya to lead them in prayer. She put down her flute and stood up. Some of the people also stood up, raising their hands in prayer, some moved from their cross-legged sitting posture to kneeling and bent forwards their heads almost touching the ground, and others remained sitting putting their hands together in front of their faces.

Freya started to pray:

"Blessed be the God and Father of our Lord Jesus Christ, who has blessed us in Christ with every spiritual blessing.

He chose us in him before the foundation of the world, that we should be holy and blameless before him.

We praise his glorious grace, which he lavished upon us, in all wisdom and insight making known to us the mystery of his will.

We recognize we have redemption through his blood, the forgiveness of sins, in order that we, who have hoped in Christ, might be for the praise of his glory."[95]

As soon as they realized what she was praying many of those present started to join in as they obviously knew the words. But then she continued in a less formal fashion and nobody followed her so Gaius realized she was making up the words – talking to God – as she went along. He found it strange that anyone should be prepared to talk to God in such an informal way but the content of what she said, which was very immediate to the concerns of the group, was wonderfully striking and appropriate.

She stopped and first one person, then another, prayed. Both men and women took part. Some spoke fluently and well; others were hesitant and quiet so he had difficulty hearing what they said. Some spoke in praise and worship; others had simple requests for health and practical things; still others prayed for other people not at the meeting. After each prayer there was a loud 'Amen'[96] or 'praise Jesus' from the congregation. More strikingly one person started praying in what seemed to be another language with lovely musical cadences to it to be followed by someone else who reported what had been said in a kind of translation.

Gaius asked Anna in a whisper what language it was. She replied that it was a prayer language spoken from the Holy Spirit and translated similarly. The prayers continued. Gaius was quite enthralled by it all.

Eventually Jacob interrupted after a gap in the prayers and suggested they should turn to scripture. Everyone returned to a sitting position and Jacob went up to the table with the scroll on it. He rolled it back from where Gaius had been reading to nearer the beginning of the scroll where he had put a linen strip in to keep the place. Even so he clearly had to hunt around to find the exact place he wanted.[97]

He read: "For God so loved the world, that he gave his one and only Son, that whoever believes in him should not perish but have eternal life. For God did not send his Son into the world to condemn the world, but in order that the world might be saved through him. Whoever believes in him is not condemned, but whoever does not believe is condemned already, because he has not believed in the name of the one and only Son of God. And this is the judgment: the light has come into the world, and people loved the darkness rather than the light because their works were evil. For everyone who does wicked things hates the light and does not come to the light, lest his works should be exposed. But whoever does what is true comes to the light, so that it may be clearly seen that his works have been carried out in God.[98]

He read the passage through slowly and with emphasis. It was in Greek, whereas so far everybody had been speaking Aramaic.

Then he read it again but this time pausing after each short sentence, translating it into Aramaic, and then explaining it in his own words, with people interrupting him and asking questions or commenting themselves.

When they came to the end of what he had read he started to read it yet again, this time pausing after each section and letting everybody repeat it after him. They went right through the passage like this; then repeated it again; and again a third time. Gaius realized that what they were doing was committing it to memory. He could see the value of that since he supposed not everybody would be able to read even if they could get access to the scrolls. This line of thought got him looking around the group of people trying to assess how many would be able to read. He reckoned he was seeing a good cross-section of the general population. Some were clearly field workers of whom he guessed the older ones would not be able to read Greek even if they could read simple Aramaic. He thought it was a good job that the scroll was not written in a literary style of Greek but in the ordinary everyday way that was widely used in the bazaars or else not many of these people would have been able to follow it and memorize it.

In the passage that had been read the words that spoke most directly to him were those that said: 'God so loved the world that he gave his one and only Son, that whoever believes in him shall not perish but have eternal life.'

Before his talks with Jacob he would not have understood how the one and only God could have a son, let alone how he could give that son in an act of loving self-sacrifice for ordinary people like himself. It was all so far away from the image of God he had had; a distant God only occasionally interested in people, their lives and loves.

He remembered too that it had said in the passage 'Light has come into the world' and 'those who live by the truth come into the light, so that it may be seen plainly that what they have done has been done in the sight of God.' He wanted to live by the truth and come into the light himself. He did not want to be evil. Good things had a strong pull on him. He wanted to come into the light.

He was uncomfortably aware that it all made good sense and was deeply attractive to him, yet at the same time, if he were to admit that it would turn his whole world upside down. He glanced sideways at Anna and wondered whether she would turn his whole world upside down anyway! It seemed a rather unworthy thought in the middle of the service so he hurriedly tried to forget it and concentrate on what was happening.

Eventually the discussion round the words that had been

read stopped, so Jacob called out, "What about our works of love and mercy this week?"

One after another individuals in the group explained what they had been doing. Gaius was amazed at how much had been done and what it was. One old lady explained how she was looking after, in her own house, an even older neighbour who was finding it difficult to survive as her husband and family had all died. She asked for help providing food and Narcissus quietly said she would provide. A young man was working the field of a neighbour who had broken his leg and was unable to work as he waited for it to mend. Two young girls were looking after the children of a couple who had the fever. There was a long list of good things that were being done by one or another of the folk there. If there were any requests for material needs it was usually Narcissus who offered to provide them. Very often, after an explanation, someone else would pray about what had been described.

Finally Jacob reminded everybody to continue to pray for the things they had heard about. Then Freya and Tigist started to play again, and everyone sang:

Jesus shall take the highest honour,
Jesus shall take the highest praise.
Let all earth join heaven in exalting
The Name which is above all other names.
Let's bow the knee in humble adoration,
For at his name every knee must bow,
Let every tongue confess he is Christ, God's only Son.
Sovereign Lord we give you glory now.[99]

As they came to the end of the song Anna, Martha and several girls got up and disappeared through to the back of the house. They reappeared very quickly carrying trays laden with bread, pieces of fish, cheese and jars of honey. They went back and brought flagons of water or wine through. They put plates with bread on and several beakers on the table that Gaius had been told was reserved for the ceremonial part of the evening. Everybody moved around forming groups of four to eight people round a tray.

Jacob stood up and called for silence. He said:

"In this so simple act of remembrance we look back to your death and resurrection, Oh Lord: make those, and the forgiveness they bring, very real to us this night.

We look forward and long for your Kingdom to come in its final glory that we may take part in the great feast of the Messiah.

We look in and see our own sin. We rejoice that your death has provided complete satisfaction for all our wrongdoings.

We look out to the world around us, our neighbours and friends, and pray that we may be good and faithful servants of you in all we do for them."

There was a chorus of deep 'Amens' as he finished. Everybody leant forward to the food in front of them, took a piece of bread and broke a small fragment off. So Gaius did too.

Everybody lifted their piece of bread above their heads, said, "The body of Jesus broken for me!" and ate together. That left Gaius perplexed as to what he should do. After a moment's thought he decided that he would do the same because he felt so very much one with all he had been told and that was going on around him. So he did, muttering the words quietly to himself as he was behind everyone else in saying them. To his astonishment as he ate his small piece of bread a strange feeling spread through him. Later when telling people about it he found it very difficult to describe what happened. It was a feeling of elation and excitement and at the same time of awe and unworthiness. He was thrilled to the very core of his being and there and then determined that he would follow Jesus.

Then someone in each group lifted a beaker of wine and

took a sip from it before passing it to the next person saying, "This is the promise of new life in him." Anna looked at him and hesitated, obviously unsure whether to pass the beaker on to him, so he reached across and took it from her with a big smile on his face. He drank and passed the beaker on to Freya who was next to him on the other side saying the same words. He didn't notice the look on Anna's face.

When they had all finished they sang, unaccompanied this time:

If we died with him, we will also live with him;

if we endure, we will also reign with him.

If we deny him, he will also deny us;

if we are faithless, he will remain faithful, for he cannot deny himself.[100]

A further chorus of 'amen' seemed to close the formal part of the meeting. Everyone relaxed and started to talk. Then Jacob's voice cut across the beginning of the conversations from the other side of the courtyard. "I think Gaius may have something to tell us," he announced. Gaius had not been aware that Jacob had been watching him closely as the bread and wine were passed around and had seen his actions and the look on his face.

Everybody stopped talking and looked across at him.

He hesitated. "I think I have just become a Christian," he said.

"What makes you say that," asked Jacob.

"Well," he paused trying to get his thoughts together. "I was getting increasingly convinced that all you told me was right and I wanted to be part of it. Then I felt a tremendous sense of being one with everything that has happened here tonight. Finally as I took the bread something happened inside me that confirmed what my mind and heart were saying. I think you – this to Jacob – would say it was the Holy Spirit coming into my life. How did you know?"

"I saw it on your face," was the simple answer. "Nathan,

I think you should continue the questioning. It is not too late at night to baptize our young friend here if you think him worthy."

A man Gaius had not noticed before nodded and spoke up. "Who do you say Jesus is?"

"I believe he is the Son of God and the Messiah and Saviour promised to us."

"What happened to him and what does it mean for you?"

"He died by crucifixion, but he rose again and was seen by many people including Jacob, here. He died that we might be forgiven and accepted by God, now and forever. I have decided to follow him so I am forgiven and accepted by God."

"What will be the consequences if you set out to follow him?"

"I don't entirely know. My family will be upset, but not too much so. In fact I think my father and mother will be quite accepting about it because I have frequently heard them talking about the Christians in our city and approving of them. I suppose in the longer term it could be a rather dangerous step to take but I will face that when I come to it. If I am in the hands of God and of Jesus I will leave the future to them." There was a murmur of approval at this statement.

"Do you know about baptism?"

"Not really. Jacob has not told me anything about that. I suppose it is the way you mark the beginning of the Christian life."

"Yes. Baptism and the gift of the Holy Spirit go together. Sixty years ago the Holy Spirit used to come on people when they were baptized. Now, he tends to come on people before they are baptized. But we try to keep the two things as close together as possible."

Nathan turned to Jacob. "Have you instructed this young man enough for him to be baptized now?"

"Yes, I have."

"Then let us go to the big pool, right now."

A mighty hubbub of voices arose as everyone stood up and prepared to move out. While conscious that Anna was close by his side through all this Gaius had not been able to see her reaction. Everybody else had seen the delight and excitement on her face at this unexpected turn of events. Many had drawn the obvious conclusion. The shadow of many mixed emotions chased each other across the face of Martha as she watched all this from the shadowed corner of the room where she had hidden herself.

Some of the men picked up the lights and started to leave. The two young men he had been talking to at the start of the meeting came up to Gaius with big smiles on their faces and asked him to follow them. Anna was quick to follow behind them. He saw that Matthew and James had joined her. Two other men took Jacob's arms to help him over the rough ground. They all filed out through the back of the house and the small gate Gaius had seen before into a dark and narrow alleyway.

11

They stumbled along the narrow alley. There were stones and dirt underfoot and an occasional doorstep sticking out into the path so progress was slow and difficult. Fortunately the alley was quite short and they came out into a more open space. Gaius was glad to see that the moon was nearly full and there was no cloud in the sky so the light was good. They soon approached a river and turned up a better path beside it. A louder noise came from the stream. It was a small waterfall beneath which was a large pool. The company assembled on the bank near to a spot where it sloped down into the water.

As they had been walking the young men with Gaius had been telling him more of what would happen so he was ready and eager for the ceremony. He kicked off his sandals and took off his outer tunic, as did Nathan who went into the water first. Gaius followed, trying not to shiver at the coldness of the water. When they were waist deep Nathan stopped and beckoned to Gaius to stand in front of him. Gaius clasped his hands together and Nathan grasped them in one of his and put his other hand behind the shoulders of Gaius.

"Gaius. Do you acknowledge your sin, and claim the forgiveness which is in Christ?" he asked.

"I do!"

"Do you accept Christ as your Saviour and Lord?"

"I do!"

"Are you prepared to follow him through whatever may be in store for you in this life in full confidence of being with him in the life to come?"

"I will!"

"On your confession of faith in him, and confidence in

his Way for you, I baptize you in the name of the Father, the Son and the Holy Spirit."

A loud 'amen' came from the assembled watchers on the bank.

Nathan pushed back on Gaius' hands swinging him down into the water, then, when he was fully submerged, he pulled up with one hand, lifted with his other hand, and swung Gaius back up to a standing position. He surfaced with a splutter and wiped his wet hair back from his eyes, revealing a big grin of pure delight on his face.

Nathan continued: "prepare your mind for action, and be sober- minded, set your hope fully on the grace that will be brought to you when Jesus Christ is revealed at his coming. As an obedient child, do not be conformed to the evil desires you had when you lived in ignorance, but as he who called you is holy, be holy in all you do, since it is written, 'You shall be holy, for I am holy.' Since you call on him as Father who judges impartially according to each one's deeds, conduct yourself with fear throughout the time you live as a foreigner, knowing that you were ransomed from the empty way of life inherited from your forefathers, not with perishable things such as silver or gold, but with the precious blood of Christ, like that of a lamb without blemish or spot.[101] Amen."

His final amen was echoed round the watchers, together with several Hallelujahs[102] and other expressions of praise and rejoicing.

Gaius came up out of the water. He looked up, straight into the eyes of Anna, who had managed to stand at the very front of the crowd. He noticed a strained look on her face and a glistening under her eyes. He only realized it was tears he was seeing when she lifted her hand to wipe them away. He was more conscious than ever of his feelings for her.

He put his dry tunic on over his wet undergarment. He

reckoned it was better to have both damp than to try to warm up in only his undergarment. There was much embracing from the men - Jacob, Matthew and James getting there first - and expressions of greeting from the women; many expressions of joy at what he had done, his commitment, and blessings for his future. But not from Anna. He wondered why.

They all walked back up the way they had come talking more than on the way down, but quietly. They were quickly back in to the courtyard and resumed the places they had left round the trays and the food. There was a great buzz of happy conversation once they were back in the house.

Jacob stood up and interrupted everybody. "This is a very happy evening for us all. But especially for me and my granddaughter, Anna. We have been talking to Gaius in great depth about the Christian Way. He has asked many sharp and important questions which we have tried to answer. I am sure he will be a great helper to many on the Way, more probably in his home city of Sidon than here. We will rejoice with our brothers and sisters there that the Lord has spoken to him in this way and he has responded so positively. We were going to eat an ordinary supper together after remembering the Lord in our accustomed way. Let this be a celebration feast as there will be rejoicing in heaven just now.[103]"

He sat down; the conversation restarted and then quickly died down as everyone reached for pieces of bread and the other good things in front of them. Near silence reigned as they ate – for a while anyway.

But before long a general hubbub of chatter broke out. Gaius looked round. In the gloom of the ill lit courtyard he had not really noticed who had sat down round the same tray of food as he and Anna had. He was delighted to see that some of the people he had been most interested in were within talking range; Narcissus, Freya, Tigist and the young man who had led the singing were all near. He received their congratulations and best wishes for a while. Then he started on some questions of his own that had been in his mind since before the interruption for his baptism.

"Where are you from?" he asked Freya.

She smiled. "I do look a bit different. That is because I come from the northern isles that the Romans call Britannia. My family were taken captive in the Roman campaign against our tribe of the Iceni about 40 years ago. Since then we have been very fortunate; we have been slaves working for the family of Narcissus." She glanced across to her mistress and friend and smiled.

"You are friends," he said next, making it sound halfway between a question and a statement. "How is it that you can play the flute so well?"

Narcissus entered the conversation. "We are careful to give our slaves the best possible education, according to their abilities. Freya is a very able person. She can also read and write. She teaches the children of our family. Tigist has care of the younger children and the babies in our household."

"And where are you from," he asked Tigist, turning towards her.

"I am Ethiopian, and a slave, and happy to be here," was the reply. "I was even a Christian in Ethiopia before I became a slave and was brought here by the family of Narcissus!"

"So there are Christians in Ethiopia?" asked Gaius. "How did that happen?"

"We had a church formed by a senior government official, the queen's financial minister, who was a very early convert to the Way of Jesus.[104] So I have been a Christian longer than anybody else in our household!"

"Good for you," was all that Gaius could think of to say

to that. He went on, "are you all in the church, then?" Obviously implying that he was surprised to see slave owners and slaves belonging to the same social grouping.

"Yes!" replied Freya with emphasis.

Narcissus spoke again, "Paul said 'There is neither Jew nor Greek, there is neither slave nor free, there is no male and female, for you are all one in Christ Jesus.'[105] He didn't say 'Jew, nor Greek neither Briton, nor Ethiopian' but I am sure we may count them in!"

"On the basis of faith," added Freya, "and no other basis. Paul said if you have given your wholehearted commitment to Jesus Messiah 'you are all sons of God through faith in Christ Jesus, for all of you who were baptized into Christ have clothed yourselves with Christ'. That is what Paul said just before he wrote the bit about us being all one in Christ Jesus."

"Clothing yourself with Christ you end up a bit damp," joked Gaius, pulling a face and tugging at his obviously damp clothes. They all laughed.

"So you are now a son of God," Narcissus pointed out with a smile. "You are in a special relationship to him and you will be an inheritor of all the promises that he has made. We are all sons, even us women, because we get an equal share in the inheritance, exactly the same as you men! No second rate inheritance for us."

There were big grins and chuckles from all four of the women at this.

"I'll get used to it. Eventually. I suppose." Gaius replied, making himself sound as uncertain as possible, but with a big grin on his face too, entering into the spirit of the occasion.

Anna spoke up. "We have been discussing the Christian faith in depth. By 'we' I mean my grandfather Jacob and the two of us."

"Oh, I see," replied Freya with something of a knowing

grin, looking at the two of them.

Gaius decided it was time to change the subject. "What did it mean in the reading from the scroll when it said something about 'not perish but have eternal life'?

It was Freya who answered, causing Gaius to realize that she was the one with the deepest grasp of the meaning of Christian faith.

"I think that is best understood by thinking about what followed in that passage. It went on to talk about the judgment day that is surely coming. When that will be we don't know. But when it will be doesn't matter, it will come.

Jesus will be the judge at that day and he will judge according to our relationship to him. We will either be accepted on the basis of our faith in him and his saving death and resurrection or we will be condemned because we have condemned ourselves by loving the darkness rather than the light.

If we are accepted now we will be accepted then, and that means we will live God honouring lives and what happens to us in this life will be a foretaste of 'eternal life'. If we are condemned we will start to perish right now and then all our lives will be a downward slide to death and the abyss. You have chosen life, in your baptism. You are accepted. You are beginning to live eternal quality life. Your problem, same as mine, same as ours, is to live up to that fact."

"Well done Freya," said Narcissus. "Jacob couldn't have put it better!"

The discussion continued between the four of them and the others round about. But it was getting late, everyone had eaten, and people were getting up saying their goodbyes – most of them came over and said special goodbyes to Gaius – and leaving.

Gaius and Anna sat in companionable silence until only they, Martha and Jacob were left.

"Would you three mind clearing up and locking up," asked Jacob. "I am feeling quite tired. It has been a good evening, a very good evening. But I am not as young as I used to be! We will talk again in the morning." This last addressed to Gaius, of course. He made his way slowly out of the courtyard.

Gaius was not used to helping women to clear up – although he had helped to set things out as they got ready – it was not part of his culture, but he was delighted at the idea of doing so with Anna and no one else around except Martha. After the so friendly and easy mixing of the men and women it seemed the natural thing to do.

They carried the trays through first. Gaius put the scroll back in its box, carried the tables back where he had got them from and picked up all the carpets and rugs they had sat upon. Then he went through to the back of the house to where Anna and Martha were rinsing the trays and plates in a big tub. He helped until they were done. They sat and talked for some time.

Gaius asked them about the people who had been present that evening. He was quite amazed at what a variety they were. Freya and Tigist were not the only slaves present; Narcissus was not the only rich slave owner. Yet he had not identified which were which very accurately, probably partly at least because they were all dressed in very ordinary clothes. He asked about this and she told him that this was deliberate policy to avoid attracting unwanted attention to themselves.

Then he turned his questioning to their family, asking where Anna's father and Martha's husband was in particular. He learnt that he had died some years ago and so Jacob and Matthew acted as joint heads of the family. It was getting late and Gaius was aware that he needed to be away early the next morning so he had to suggest that they should part and go to bed.

Chapter 11

It was with great pleasure that he said, "The Lord be with you" as they parted. He had heard that it was the common farewell expression in use amongst the Christians. He got a lovely smile and a reciprocal, "And with your spirit," from Anna.

He was up, had breakfast and was ready to go, early the next morning. He had to explain to Anna that he would not be able to call on the way past on his way back as he expected to be with a caravan taking papyrus reed to Sidon but he would hope to visit again before too long.

Jacob told him which way to go to make an early connection with a caravan going on to Caesarea. They said their good-byes. Gaius was left thinking that they were saying 'good-bye' rather too often. He wished it was not necessary.

12

Back in Sidon, a week later Gaius was surprised to receive a parcel brought to him at the workshop by one of the town's messenger boys. When he asked who it was from he was told the boy had been given it by a man with a train of mules who had not given his name. He unwrapped it carefully, wondering what it could possibly be. At first he thought it was a papyrus scroll but then he realized it was in several pieces all closely covered with writing. One of them looked very like the new piece of papyrus he had given to Jacob and Anna. There was a small piece of papyrus, obviously a note, with them. He read:

Jacob and Anna, servants of the Lord, to Gaius. Grace to you and peace in the Lord Jesus. This is part of the Gospel according to John. It is about the first third of the gospel, and the last third, which is all we could get on the papyrus we had available and, we thought, the most important bits for you. We will send the rest when we can get the papyrus for it. We hope your work with the new papyrus materials is going well. The grace of Christ Jesus be with you.

With great delight he found the start of the scroll and read: "In the beginning was the Word, and the Word was with God, and the Word was God. He was with God in the beginning. Through him all things were made; without him nothing was made that has been made. In him was life, and that life was the light of men. The light shines in the darkness, but the darkness has not understood it."[106]

He called his father and read these words to him. That evening his father got him to read a great deal more until it was so dark that even with a good lamp his eyes were too tired to read any more.

He wondered greatly who in such a small village had

been able to copy a scroll so well. He took advantage of the fact that his father was so clearly impressed with what he had read to ask him if he might go back up to see Anna and Jacob and told him what he proposed to do.

So it was after their evening meal the following day that Anna, Martha and Jacob heard again a thunderous knocking on their gate, beating out the same rhythm as before. So Anna knew why she was running to open the gate.

Gaius was delighted to see her bright eyes and quick flush. Anna noted his dancing eyes. They greeted each other formally, and then he went in to greet Jacob and Martha.

"A horse this time!" commented Jacob.

"Yes. I am only coming as far as here. I need to go back to Sidon tomorrow and I need to be able to do it quickly if I am going to have any time here tomorrow morning. I wanted to come and see you all."

Jacob wondered whether the 'all' was actually correct or rather misleading.

Anna hurried to get him something to eat, which he had as soon as he had stabled the horse. As he ate they asked him about the papyrus business and he reported that it was going well. That led him to the obvious question: "That was a wonderful gift you sent me. Where did you get it from? I thought you only had the one copy of the gospel here."

"We had," replied Jacob. "so we copied it, at least as much of it as we could. Our scroll wasn't long enough for the whole gospel."

"You copied it!" Gaius said, the rising intonation of his voice expressing his surprise better than any words could have done. "Who copied it? That is a very difficult job. I know because we have started to do some copying of documents ourselves. It is not at all easy. Who copied it?"

He looked round at the others and noticed immediately

that Anna was studying her toenails very intently.

Jacob said, "Anna, of course, Anna!"

"You did this!" This was said to Anna. "You wrote all this! You can write this well. You can write well enough to do this. It's wonderful. I didn't realize you could read and write as well as this. It's marvellous. You are so clever. Wait till my dad hears about this and sees you. He will be thrilled to bits."

Which last comment presupposed several things not yet said. The conversation went on about copying documents and scrolls for quite some time. Before very long it was time for bed. Jacob and Martha glanced at each other and walked away without a word leaving Anna and Gaius still talking at the table.

When the older folk were safely out of the way Gaius plucked up his courage and took the initiative.

"Anna," he said, not quite in his usual easy way. She thought she knew what was coming. "What would you say if I was to ask your grandfather if I might marry you?"

He felt her hand steal across and hold his tight, which was as good as an answer.

"Gaius, we have only known each other for about a month, but the answer is 'YES'. I fell in love with you almost as soon as I saw you. But are you not already betrothed or married to a girl in Sidon."

He sighed. "I was married but my wife died in childbirth nearly two years ago. So did the child. It was very sad." He paused.

Anna hesitantly asked, "Did you love her? That must have been very hard."

"It was. I think it was actually harder because I didn't love her very much. It was an arranged marriage. We seemed a good match for each other but somehow it never really worked very well. I think I was looking for someone vigorous and outgoing, someone who would be a real friend as well as a wife and Julia was a quiet girl who wanted to be with her girlfriends all the time and didn't seem to have much time for me. We just didn't have much in common. That really made her death harder because I kept on thinking of what I should have done differently and better to make it a good marriage. But I didn't, and it wasn't."

He stopped, looking sad. Anna did not know what to say so wisely said nothing.

"As a result," he continued, "my father has told me they will not choose another wife for me but will leave me to choose one for myself. I think you are all the things poor Julia was not. I couldn't even tell you this when you told me about the tragedy in your life when your fiancé was killed. It was too difficult. But now I must. This is why I am considerably older than most unmarried men. In the ordinary way my parents might have been quite upset at me wanting to marry a girl who is a Christian from a small village like this but I read a lot of the gospel to them last night and I am sure they will not be upset. In fact when they meet you and see how well you can write I think they will be totally delighted."

He turned and looked squarely at Anna. "It is yes, then!"

"Oh, yes, it certainly is."

He reached round to hug her. She responded for a moment but then pushed him away. "We mustn't," she said. "We need to wait. How long will we have to wait? I don't want to wait the traditional one year. Will we have to?"

"No. I don't think so. We are both a bit older than is usual for betrothal and marriage so I think we should be able to speed things up. I will have to go home and tell my parents the outcome of this visit although I have already told my father what I was proposing to do. My parents and your family will want to negotiate the dowry.[107] My folk are quite well off and are likely to be generous when they hear your father has died. When that is agreed I will come back, or I may come back with their reply even before it is all agreed. When I do come back you will be all ready to come back to Sidon with me, won't you?"

"Oh yes. I don't know what it will be like. The only time I have been in a city it was on a visit to Damascus. I must say I didn't really like it all that much. Is Sidon as big as that?"

"No. but it is a fairly big place. We live on the edge of the city in what used to be a village so it is not going to be too difficult for you."

They went on talking for a long time through the night. They told each other more about their families than they had before. Gaius described in detail where they would be living, his work, and his hopes for what their future might be. As they talked, they slowly got closer and closer together with Anna snuggled close into Gaius and his arm round her.

Finally she said, with a slight giggle, "We had better go to our beds before the sun comes up and my mother and grandfather wake up and wonder what we have been up to all night! But we need to do it very quietly."

Gaius reluctantly took his arm away but managed to retain hold of her hand as long as possible as they walked through to where they slept. As they parted he pulled Anna to him, not that she was at all reluctant, and they kissed. Finally Anna stood back, put her finger to his lips to keep them closed and quiet and left him.

Gaius went to his bed and lay down. But it was a long time before he fell asleep as he thought of all that had happened and thrilled to the prospect of what lay before him, or rather, them.

13

Gaius woke to the sound of heavy knocking on the door of the room. "Hello!" he shouted.

"Time to get up – long past time to get up," came through the door from Anna.

Then it all came flooding back into his mind, all that had happened the previous day and half the night. He had probably never got off his bed faster in his life than he did that morning. In one bound he was at the door, had it open, and grasped Anna.

"Shhh!" she hissed in his ear gesturing along the verandah towards the courtyard. "Grandpa has been up a long time. He is just round the corner, and I don't know whether he would approve of us showing affection in front of him."

She wished that she could hug and kiss him. She thought how good it would have been if they could just sit, cuddle and chat with each other. However, she knew she could not do that because her grandpa was not far away. And she was not even sure that her mother and brothers approved of Gaius. All sorts of thoughts were pulling her first this way and then that.

"Oh!" said Gaius, letting her go reluctantly. "Am I late? Aren't you tired? I lay awake for a very long time trying to think of what would happen and what I – I mean we – could do. I had what I think is a very good idea. I just hope your grandfather approves of it."

"I do want to hear. Very much. But you must come through and have your breakfast immediately. Then you can tell me."

Gaius got himself ready very quickly and went through to where they usually ate. He had no sooner sat down than

Jacob appeared.

"Good morning," he said as he sat down opposite Gaius. "You had a good day yesterday. Or" - there was a rare twinkle in his eye at this point – "did you perchance have an even more exciting evening than I know about?"

Gaius stared at him. "Have you guessed?" he asked.

"Guessed?" asked Jacob teasingly. "What would I have to guess about?"

Gaius laughed. "You have guessed," he decided.

"Stop talking in riddles and tell me what I might have guessed then."

Gaius then blurted out. "I want to marry Anna. I asked her last night if I might ask you and her family if that could be arranged and she was very happy at the idea. Please, can we get married? I know my parents are a full day's journey away but I can take letters back and I am sure my father would be prepared to come here if necessary."

Jacob paused for a moment, though the look on his face certainly suggested he was not unhappy about the idea.

"I think that is possible. The way we are situated here Anna's mother, and her brothers, need to be consulted. But, although I have only known you for a very short time I am prepared to recommend that you be allowed to do so." Then he shouted, " Anna!"

"Yes, grandpa?" A rather hesitant face appeared round the corner.

"Come here!" He reached up and put his arm round her waist in an unusual gesture of affection. "I shall be so sad to lose you, but I could not possibly stand in the way of what you want to do."

"You mean …. You mean ….."

"You are not usually lost for words, girl! Yes, I do mean - I would be happy to give you my blessing to marry this fellow, though I really know so little about him. He seems to have captured my heart as well as yours."

Chapter 13

Anna tried to look as though she was unhappy at the thought of leaving him and her home to go and live with a comparative stranger, but failed badly. "Oh, grandpa" He got a big kiss on first one cheek and then the other. However, she quickly realized that she should have not been quite so boldly expressive before her grandfather. She blushed and did not know how to cover the situation.

"Steady up, girl. We will have to talk to your mother and your brothers before we go any further."

Anna spun round to face Gaius who had watched all this with a big smile on his face. "But they are not likely to contradict grandpa! Oh, I'm so excited I think I'm going to burst! I do wish I didn't have to be so quiet and modest about it. I want to shout it from the roof tops, but I mustn't!"

"What about calling your mother through and bringing us something through to celebrate," suggested Jacob.

Anna disappeared at high speed and reappeared quickly with her mother, a tray, four beakers, food and drinks. Gaius realized she must have had them all ready. It was immediately obvious that Martha knew all about what they had agreed anyway. The beakers were filled and they ate and drank to celebrate the future of the young couple. Jacob and Martha were probably more aware than Gaius and Anna were of just what problems might lie ahead of them in such uncertain times for declared Christians, but they knew that whatever might happen to them they would rejoice one day in the presence of their Lord and King, Jesus.

They chatted for a while. Gaius repeated much of what he had told Anna during the night about his family, their house and where they lived.

Jacob asked, "What do you do in your father's workshop? You have talked of being well educated. Have you finished studying and started working full time?"

Gaius hesitated. "Yes, and there is something I really

wanted to talk about. I had a strange idea in the night. Perhaps it was the Holy Spirit talking to me again. I don't know how to put this. It may sound very mercenary but I certainly don't mean it that way." He hesitated again. The others leaned forward wondering what was coming.

"I was very interested to see your scroll last week. You see, my father has just a small business and I have been working with him for the last year. He started importing papyrus from Egypt many years ago and selling it locally. Then, quite recently, he started making papyrus himself. He had an awful job finding out how to do it because the Egyptians treat it as a secret and try to stop anyone else learning how to do it. My journeys to find and buy papyrus reed were all part of that work.

Then even more recently we have started copying scrolls as well, in a small way, and that is what I am mostly involved in. When I saw your gospel scroll I was very interested, not only in what it contained but in how it was written and the quality of the material and the writing.

Then during last night I had a quite unexpected idea. You would think I would have spent all my time thinking about Anna and our future life together but it didn't work out that way. I thought we could perhaps copy gospels and the other documents you have mentioned – letters of Paul wasn't it? By having one person reading from the scroll being copied and several others writing down what he said we could do more, more accurately and cheaper.

There is something else too. Have you ever heard of a codex?"

Jacob and Anna looked puzzled. "What is that?" asked Anna.

"Instead of writing on a scroll you write on small rectangles of papyrus. Several of these are folded down the middle and stitched together with a leather cord. Then you write on them first here and then there"

He demonstrated with his hands how they would be and the order in which they would be written on.[108]

"It would be much easier to find the place you wanted in a codex than in a scroll. Remember what a job you had finding the bit you wanted last week at the meeting when I had been reading from further through the scroll? With a codex you would remember which page you wanted and whereabouts on the page the bit you wanted was. Much easier."

"That is quite an idea, young man," said Jacob. He continued with a smile to take any possible sting out of his words, "I am glad you had this idea after you had made your profession of faith and been baptized or I might have wondered whether you had seen the business opportunity first! What do you think?" This last addressed to Anna.

"It sounds like a very good idea, grandpa. It would be so nice for people in fellowships in small villages like this to have copies of all the gospels and some of Paul's letters."

"I think you said there are four gospels," said Gaius with a query in his voice.

"Yes, that's right. Well there are more," Jacob admitted, "but none of them except the four are accepted as reliable accounts. And now there are next to no eye-witnesses left – I am one of the very last – there is no chance of there being anymore."

"Is it being an eye-witness that is most important?"

"Yes. One of the apostles who was with Jesus throughout his three year ministry, Matthew by name, wrote one of the gospels. Another gospel, the one that we read from at the meeting, was written by people very close to another of the apostles called John following closely his recollections of his time with Jesus; a third was written by John Mark following the account given him by Peter, the leader of the apostles; the fourth was written by a doctor called Luke who spent a lot of time researching what actually happened with eye-witnesses of the events. What he wrote is more history than the others, which are life stories of Jesus.[109] We know these gospels as 'the gospel according to Matthew' or Mark, or Luke, or John, though none of them have actually put their names to the scrolls because they want all the attention to focus on Jesus."

"Why has nobody put them all together into one account? Surely that would be the most sensible thing to do?"

"Yes, and no. That has been discussed very carefully. I took part in some of the early meetings but I am not able to travel now. But I do get reports from people passing through and I thoroughly agree with what has been decided. Each of these four - Evangelists as we call them - has written his account in such a way as to bring out specific things in the life of Jesus. They have written their accounts to teach different things to their readers. So it has been decided that these stories should be left as they have written them. They had a huge number of possible incidents they could have reported on and they had to make choices. Of course, there are differences, as there are bound to be when you are reporting a story of what happened rather than setting down a list of instructions or statements."

"If there are differences how can you think of these writings as authoritative or God given, as I assume you would want to do? Oops! I guess I should have said WE will want to do!"

Jacob chuckled. "You have got a very astute young man here Anna," he said.

"We do understand that these are God given. Paul once said they are God-breathed, breathed out by God. That means they are the words that the Lord wanted us to have even if one account varies a little from the next. After all your story of what happened last night will, I am sure, be rather different from Anna's! But that doesn't make either of your stories any the less true."

Gaius and Anna chuckled.

"We believe that what the Bible says does not mislead us. It doesn't even need a trained expert to correctly understand what it means. But we also recognize that even after the words are written we do still have to understand them. The process of us understanding what has been written and what God wants us to do as a result is not complete until we have correctly understood what is written. We have to interpret the writings and that is never a completely straightforward business even when we have the Holy Spirit to help us. As I said these are stories of what actually happened as seen and reported by eyewitnesses and stories can be misunderstood."

"Yes, I see what you mean," said Gaius thoughtfully. He went on, "The words of God to Moses were written down in stone and are easy to understand because they were not reports but commands. You are saying that things are different when you are reporting on events that actually happened. I see that. To ask another question: are these writings translated?"

"Yes. Of course. We don't venerate the writings; we venerate their meaning. The words used are much less important than the message they convey. To us what they say and what they mean are all important. Why? Are you beginning to think about getting translations done now?"

Gaius laughed. "I think that would be a step too far. As yet, anyway. You must have people making translations already. Are all the writings in Greek? Or are some of them in Hebrew or Aramaic?"

"They are all in Greek. In fact they are in part already translations since Jesus spoke mainly in Aramaic. I am not an expert in Greek but I am told that the standard of the Greek varies considerably from one writing to another depending on who wrote them and how well educated they were. That does occasionally cause a problem, as sometimes some scribes like to improve the Greek as they copy. We try to discourage that, believing that the documents everybody has should be as accurate copies of the originals as possible. Whatever anyone may say it is never possible to have completely accurate copies of any document but we are managing to get everybody to keep a very high standard.

You see we believe that Jesus was, among other things, the Word of God. He was God speaking to us. That has never happened before and it will never happen again. Because Jesus was the Word of God he is the final revelation of God to men. In the past God spoke through the great prophets but only one man has been God and able to speak as God. Never again will there be prophets like the prophets there have been. Also because Jesus was the Word of God we worship him and not any written words. He is above all prophets and all writings."

When he stopped Anna broke into the conversation, addressing Gaius, "Aren't you hungry," she said. "You haven't had any breakfast yet and if you don't have it soon it will be time for the midday meal."

"Go and do as you are told!" said Jacob with a laugh. "It may be the first time but it won't be the last!"

14

The rest of the morning until Gaius had to leave turned into a bit of a festival. Matthew and James were away on a trip but their wives, Rebekah and Sarah, and, of course, the children came round. There was happy chaos in the courtyard.

Jacob asked Anna to come with him as scribe and they disappeared for a while, coming back with a note for the father of Gaius. This was given to Gaius. They told him that Matthew would be visiting his family the next time he was in Sidon to make arrangements for the wedding. He was, of course, also going to check out that everything that Gaius had told them was true, but they did not tell Gaius that. He guessed it would be so anyway.

As lunch time approached Anna manoeuvred Gaius and herself away into a side room and suggested that they should pray together before they had to separate. They knelt side by side. Gaius, having no experience of small ad hoc prayer meetings, wondered what to do but decided, male though he might be, he should leave the initiative to Anna. After all, her ability to take a lead in situations like this was one of the things that had attracted him to her so strongly.

"Listen to this," she said. "This is one of the things Paul wrote. It is lovely.

"If I speak in the tongues of men and of angels, but have not love, I am a noisy gong or a clanging cymbal. And if I have prophetic powers, and understand all mysteries and all knowledge, and if I have all faith, so as to remove mountains, but have not love, I am nothing. If I give away all I have, and if I deliver up my body to be burned, but have not love, I gain nothing. Love is patient and kind; love does not envy or boast; it is not arrogant or rude. It does not insist on its own way; it is not irritable or resentful; it does not rejoice at wrongdoing, but rejoices with the truth. Love bears all things, believes all things, hopes all things, and endures all things. Love never ends."[110]

Paul was writing about love in a general sense, not about the love between a man and a woman, but it is good isn't it?"

"Yes," said Gaius. "But love between a man and woman is about the most important sort of love there is so it does tell us how we should live together in a very powerful way. I hope I will always be – what was it – patient and kind, not angry or rude. That won't be easy however much I love you."

"Or for me," retorted Anna. "It won't be easy for either of us but since we start off together walking in the Way of Jesus it will be much easier than it would otherwise be."

She took his hand. "Come let us pray."

So they knelt together pouring out their joy and excitement at all that had happened to them since they met.

Eventually Anna raised his hand to her lips, kissed it, and got up. "Come," she said. "We must join the others."

They found that the table was laid with as good a feast as Martha and the two young mothers could get together in the time available. The sense of festival continued as they ate and rejoiced together. All too soon it was time for Gaius to go if he was to have any hope of reaching Sidon before dark.

He walked with Anna to the edge of the village, leading the horse and talking all the way. There they said goodbye to each other. Gaius assured Anna one last time that he would soon be back and that the dowry was not likely to be any problem at all. They managed a quick kiss and a hug, not too obviously, before they parted.

Gaius started off down the road setting his horse to a

Chapter 14

steady ground eating canter. When he reached the first bend in the road round an outcrop of rock he turned and looked back. He could just see Anna standing watching him go. They waved to each other.

They had much to celebrate. Gaius had placed his faith and trust in the hands of the only true God, the God who, in the person of Jesus, had visited this earth, died on the cross and risen again. The resurrection of Jesus, a sure act of history, established beyond doubt that he was who he claimed to be. Gaius could do nothing other than believe the account Jacob had given him of the events in which he had been involved even if only on the edge of the main group of believers at the most important moments.

Gaius and Anna were going to set out on their life together on the best possible basis: a shared faith in which love was the preeminent virtue and in which respect for the other was regarded as the essential service required of those who would be righteous.

No wonder they were rejoicing.

Afterword

To get more insight into the Christian Way access the Partakers internet site. It is maintained by my friend and the editor of this book, Dave Roberts. He changes it every day using material he is sent from all sorts of places all round the world by all sorts of people. It is well worth a daily visit.

More information is available on the page opposite.

Roger

About Partakers

Vision Statement: Partakers exists to communicate and disseminate resources for the purposes of Christian Discipleship, Evangelism and Worship by employing radical and relevant methods, including virtual reality and online distribution.

Mission Statement: To help the world, one person at a time, to engage in whole life discipleship, as Partakers of Jesus Christ.

Contact us to see how we can help you. Seminars, coaching, preaching, teaching, discipleship or evangelism – offline or online.

Email: dave@partakers.co.uk
Mobile: 0794 794 5511
Website: http://www.partakers.co.uk

References

[1] Assuming he died in 33 AD, the most likely year.

[2] A Rabbi was a Jewish teacher of the Law of Moses, which they called the Torah.

[3] Caesarea Philippi in the upper Jordan valley

[4] John 14: 6

[5] A boy is mentioned in one Gospel as giving his loaves and fishes to the disciples for Jesus to use. Nothing else is known about him.

[6] Mark 15: 42   It was Preparation Day (that is, the day before the Sabbath)...... .

[7] After these things Joseph of Arimathea, who was a disciple of Jesus, but secretly for fear of the Jews, asked Pilate that he might take away the body of Jesus, and Pilate gave him permission. So he came and took away his body. Nicodemus also came ... the place where he was crucified there was a garden, and in the garden a new tomb in which no one had yet been laid. So because of the Jewish day of Preparation, since the tomb was close at hand, they laid Jesus there

[8] Mark 16: 1   When the Sabbath was past, Mary Magdalene, Mary the mother of James, and Salome bought spices so that they might go and anoint him.

[9] John 20: 14 – 16   Having said this, she turned around and saw Jesus standing, but she did not know that it was Jesus. Jesus said to her, "Woman, why are you weeping? Whom are you seeking?" Supposing him to be the gardener, she said to him, "Sir, if you have carried him away, tell me where you have laid him, and I will take him away." Jesus said to her, "Mary." She turned and said to him in Aramaic, "Rabboni!" (which means Teacher

[10] Luke 24: 1, 9 – 11   But on the first day of the week, at early dawn, they went to the tomb, taking the spices they had prepared ... returning from the tomb they told all these things to the eleven and to all the rest. Now it was Mary Magdalene and Joanna and Mary the mother of James and the other women with them who told these things to the apostles, but these words seemed to

them an idle tale, and they did not believe them.

[11] John 20: 3 – 8 So Peter went out with the other disciple, and they were going toward the tomb. Both of them were running together, but the other disciple outran Peter and reached the tomb first. And stooping to look in, he saw the linen cloths lying there, but he did not go in. Then Simon Peter came, following him, and went into the tomb. He saw the linen cloths lying there, and the face cloth, which had been on Jesus ' head, not lying with the linen cloths but folded up in a place by itself. Then the other disciple, who had reached the tomb first, also went in, and he saw and believed

[12] Reported by Paul in his letter to the church in Corinth 1 Corinthians 15: 6

[13] John 20: 29 "Have you believed because you have seen me? Blessed are those who have not seen and yet have believed

[14] John 19: 34 one of the soldiers pierced his side with a spear, and at once there came out blood and water

[15] Luke 24: 16, 31 But their eyes were kept from recognizing him .... And their eyes were opened, and they recognized him

[16] Luke 4: 28 - 30

[17] John 8: 59

[18] John 18: 4 - 12

[19] Luke 24: 40 When he had said this, he showed them his hands and feet.

[20] John 20: 19, 26 On the evening of that day, the first day of the week, the doors being locked where the disciples were for fear of the Jews, Jesus came and stood among them and said to them, "Peace be with you' ..... Eight days later, his disciples were inside again, and Thomas was with them. Although the doors were locked, Jesus came and stood among them.

[21] Modern France

[22] Modern Iraq and Iran

[23] The ruins are in the valley in the mountains behind Taxila near Islamabad, Pakistan

[24] In modern south-west India

[25] Watered wine was the common drink in those countries in those days, being all that was safe to drink.

[26] Genesis 1: 1

[27] Genesis 1: 26, 27; 2: 7

[28] Psalm 89: 26 "He shall cry to me, 'You are my Father, my God...'"

[29] Genesis 12: 2,3

[30] 2 Chronicles 10: 7

[31] Genesis 18: 22 - 33

[32] Genesis 32: 24 - 32

[33] Exodus 34: 29, 30

[34] Exodus 33: 11

[35] Psalm 23

[36] Exodus 20

[37] Letter to the Galatians 3: 26 - 29

[38] From a Jewish perspective

[39] John 18: 36

[40] Isaiah 42: 1 - 4

[41] Isaiah 61: 1, 2

[42] Luke 4: 21

[43] Isaiah 53: 3

[44] Exodus 34: 6, 7

[45] Deuteronomy 6: 4,5

[46] 1 Corinthians 8: 6

[47] Genesis 18: 1, 2, 6, 16, 17, 33, 19: 1, 2

[48] Genesis 1: 2

[49] Proverbs 8: 29, 30

[50] Titus 1: 4

[51] John 16: 7

[52] Exodus 3: 14

[53] Isaiah 43: 12, 13

[54] John 6: 20 translated as 'it is I'

[55] John 8: 58

[56] John 8: 59

[57] Matthew 5: 21, 22

58 Matthew 5: 27, 28

59 Genesis 1: 27; 2: 7

60 Genesis 2: 17; 3: 6,7

61 Genesis 4: 8

62 Genesis 6 - 8

63 Babylon,

64 Genesis 11: 1 - 9

65 Gen 12: 2,3

66 Judges 21: 25

67 Amos 2: 6, 7

68 Isaiah 5: 13, 15, 16

69 Isaiah 8: 7, 8

70 Leviticus 16: 5 – 10, 15 - 22

71 Mark 10: 45

72 Matthew 26: 28

73 Acts 2: 38

74 Acts 3: 19

75 Romans 6: 5

76 Romans 3: 10

77 John 5: 22, 25, 27

78 Daniel 7: 13, 14

79 Deuteronomy 6: 4, 5

80 Leviticus 19: 18

81 Mark 12: 29 – 31   "The most important one," answered Jesus, "is this: 'Hear, O Israel, the Lord our God, the Lord is one. Love the Lord your God with all your heart and with all your soul and with all your mind and with all your strength.' The second is this: 'Love your neighbour as yourself.' There is no commandment greater than these."

82 Mark 3: 4   Then Jesus asked them, "Which is lawful on the Sabbath: to do good or to do evil, to save life or to kill?"

83 Mark 2: 27   Then he said to them, "The Sabbath was made for man, not man for the Sabbath."

84 Matthew 15: 11, 16 "it is not what goes into the mouth that defiles a person, but what comes out of the mouth; this defiles a person." "Are you also still without understanding? Do you not see that whatever goes into the mouth passes into the stomach and is expelled? But what comes out of the mouth proceeds from the heart, and this defiles a person. For out of the heart come evil thoughts, murder, adultery, sexual immorality, theft, false witness, slander. These are what defile a person. But to eat with unwashed hands does not defile anyone"

85 Romans 14: 3

86 2 Corinthians 12: 20

87 Galatians 5: 22, 23

88 John 14: 15, 26; 15: 26; 16: 7. John 16: 7 But I tell you the truth: It is for your good that I am going away. Unless I go away, the Helper will not come to you; but if I go, I will send him to you. (The Greek word for the Holy Spirit is *paracletos*, which is hard to translate into English. Possibilities are: Helper, Advocate, Counsellor, Comforter, one called alongside to help).

89 John 3: 3 "Truly, truly, I say to you, unless one is born again he cannot see the kingdom of God.

90 John 15: 5 "I am the vine; you are the branches. Whoever abides in me and I in him, he it is that bears much fruit; apart from me you can do nothing.

91 John 7: 37, 38 Jesus stood up and cried out, "If anyone thirsts, let him come to me and drink. Whoever believes in me, as the Scripture has said, 'Out of his heart will flow rivers of living water'"

92 Greek was written without spaces between words or even paragraphs so it was very difficult to find a particular passage in the middle of a scroll.

93 John 11: 1 – 3

94 1 Timothy 3: 16. Almost certainly a quotation from a song well known in the churches.

95 Taken from Ephesians 1: 3 - 12

96 'Amen' is an old word meaning 'so be it'.

97 No chapters or verses, or gaps in the manuscript in those days.

References

[98] John 3: 16 - 21

[99] Part of a modern song closely based on Philippians 2: 9,10

[100] 2 Timothy 2: 11 – 13 which is probably part of an old hymn from those days.

[101] Taken from 1 Peter 1: 13 - 19

[102] Praise the Lord (literally praise Yahweh)

[103] Luke 15: 7

[104] Acts 8: 27 - 39

[105] Galatians 3: 28

[106] John 1: 1 - 5

[107] A dowry in those days was paid from the groom's family to the bride's. More like a bride's price therefore.

[108] Like a book. The very first of these came in about this time. It is thought that Christians were the first people to make full use of the idea.

[109] Luke 1: 1 – 4 Many have undertaken to draw up an account of the things that have been fulfilled among us, just as they were handed down to us by those who from the first were eyewitnesses and servants of the word. Therefore, since I myself have carefully investigated everything from the beginning it seemed good to me to write an orderly account for you, most excellent Theophilus, that you may have certainty concerning the things you have been taught.

[110] 1 Corinthians 13: 1 – 8

13792503R00081

Printed in Great Britain
by Amazon.co.uk, Ltd.,
Marston Gate.